THE BOY WHO BIKED THE WORLD

Part Three: Riding Home through Asia

ALASTAIR HUMPHREYS
ILLUSTRATED BY TOM MORGAN-JONES

Published by Eye Books

Published in 2015
by Eye Books
29 Barrow Street
Much Wenlock
Shropshire
TF13 6EN
www.eye-books.com

ISBN: 978-1-78563-008-8

Copyright © Alastair Humphreys, 2015
Illustrations copyright © Tom Morgan-Jones, 2015

Typeset in Walsh and Optima. Journal typeface based on Grace McCarthy-Steed's handwriting.
Counting in Chinese on One Hand image sourced from Wikipedia.
Georgian Alaphabet sourced from UCLU Georgian Society.
Flags sourced from activityvillage.co.uk; colouringbook.org; coloringkids.org; flags-to-print.com

The moral right of the author has been asserted. All rights reserved. No part of this publication may be reproduced, stored in a retrieval system, or transmitted, in any form or by any means without the prior written permission of the publisher, nor be otherwise circulated in any form of binding or cover other than that in which it is published and without a similar condition being imposed on the subsequent purchaser.

British Library Cataloguing in Publication Data.
A catalogue record for this book is available from the British Library.

Printed by CPI Group (UK) Ltd, Croydon CR0 4YY

For George and Sophie

Contents

Battling Snow in Siberia	9
Half a World Away	15
Pancakes and Reindeer	23
Riding the Wild Winter Road	29
Steaming through Japan	39
Tokyo Tower Blocks, Temples and Mount Fuji	45
Chaos and Chopsticks in China	53
Beijing to the Great Wall	61
The Taklamakan Desert	71
Cycling the Stans	79
Nomads along the Silk Road	87
Goodbye Asia, Hello Europe	97
Pedal Power and the Final Push	105
Round the World and Home Again	115
Find Out and Colour In – Flags	122
Your Adventure Journal	124
Acknowledgements	126
About Eye Books	127
About the Author	128

USA
Canada
USA
Central America
BOOK TWO
South America
UK

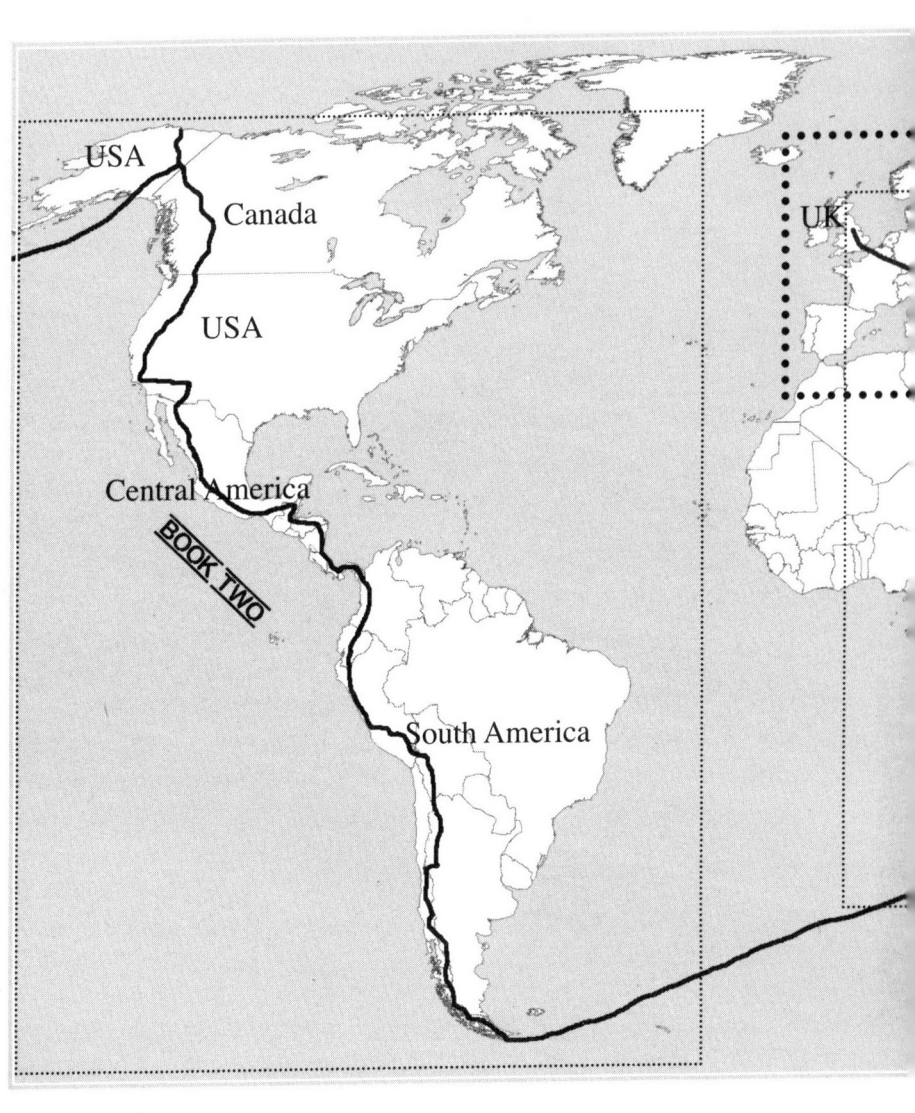

Tom's Route Round the World

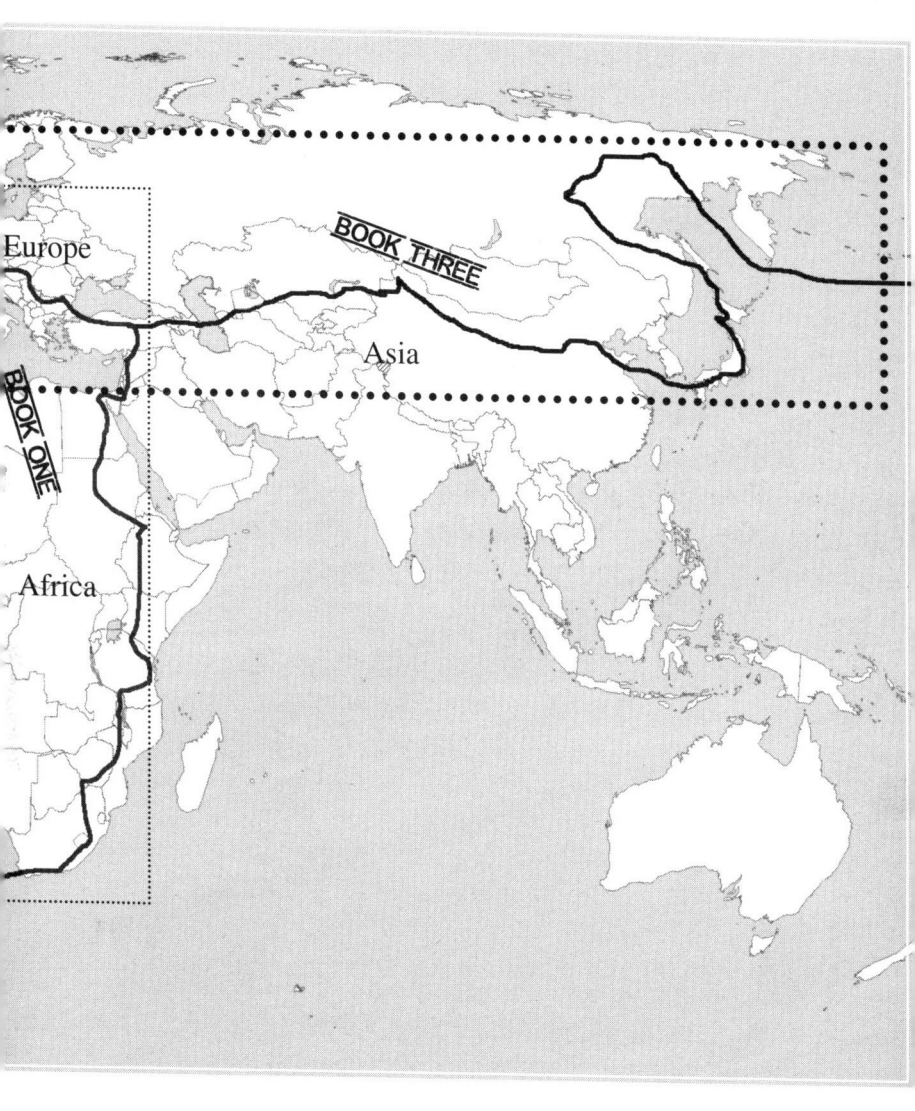

Battling Snow in Siberia

Tom was cold. He was shivering. And he was frightened. He was going faster and faster. Trees passed in a blur. He couldn't stop. This was going to end badly. But it was supposed to have been fun! Riding your bike downhill is fun. In fact, it was one of Tom's favourite things to do. But this was not fun. This was no fun at all.

Tom was about to crash. He was flying down a big hill at top speed – in deep snow. His brakes could not stop him. Tom loved sledging, but this was ridiculous. All he could do was hang on tight! Waiting for the crash was almost worse than the crash itself was going to feel.

It was time for Tom's last option. To scream.

"Aaaaagggghhhhhhhh! Help!"

But nobody could help. Nobody even heard him scream. Tom was alone. He was hundreds of miles from the nearest human. Siberia is one of the emptiest places in the world. And, in winter, it is one of the coldest, too. Nobody was bonkers enough to be outside in this weather. Nobody except Tom.

Siberia is a huge region of Russia famous for its ferocious winters. Tom was trying to cycle across Siberia in the middle of winter. Everyone had told him it was a crazy idea. Maybe they were right after all ...

CRASH!

SPLAT!

Tom landed face down in a snowdrift. For a minute or two, he did not move. He was not sure if he was broken or not. Then, ever so slowly, Tom wiggled his toes. Then his fingers. Then his nose. Everything seemed to be in place. The snow had cushioned his fall. Tom was OK. But lying face down in freezing snow is not a nice feeling, so Tom slowly pulled himself upright.

Falling off your bike is horrible. Getting a load of snow down the back of your neck isn't nice either. But Tom was lucky this time and was not injured. As he stood up he left behind in the snowdrift a splatted-Tom-shaped hole that made him chuckle.

"Maybe I really am crazy," Tom said to himself. "Everyone says I am. I'm out here, in the middle of nowhere, on my own, on a bike, in the middle of winter. I've crashed on every hill I've ridden down today. This is stupid. It's stupid, but it's brilliant!"

Tom smiled as he hauled his crashed bike from the snowdrift, struggling as it was really heavy. Tom was carrying all the equipment he needed to cycle round the world. And in winter, in Siberia, that meant a lot of gear.

The young cyclist stamped his feet and whirled his arms like a windmill. It's the best way to warm your hands when they are freezing cold. Then he climbed back onto his bike.

The Boy Who Biked the World

This was tricky too, as the multiple layers of clothes – now soggy and damp – weighed a ton.

Here is what Tom was wearing:

- 2 pairs of long thermal underwear, like pyjamas
- Trousers
- 2 fleeces
- Windproof jacket and trousers to keep off the wind. Wind chill is what makes you the coldest
- A big puffy duvet jacket for when not pedalling
- A thin balaclava
- A woolly hat
- Thin gloves for fiddly jobs to stop fingers sticking to frozen metal
- Thicker gloves
- Huge mittens
- A big Russian fur hat
- Thin socks
- Two pairs of thick socks
- Warm Russian felt boots called *valenki*

Tom had also covered the saddle of his bike with a layer of reindeer fur to keep his bottom warm! One advantage of wearing so many clothes was that they cushioned him each time he skidded and crashed on the snow and ice.

But nobody said that cycling round the world was going to be easy. In fact, most people said it would be impossible. Tom knew that if he was going to become the boy who biked the world then he'd have to make it through a lot of hard times like this.

And as he pedalled away down that long, silent, empty road through the snowy forest, Tom began to whistle a cheerful tune.

RIDING HOME THROUGH ASIA - THE LAST LEG!

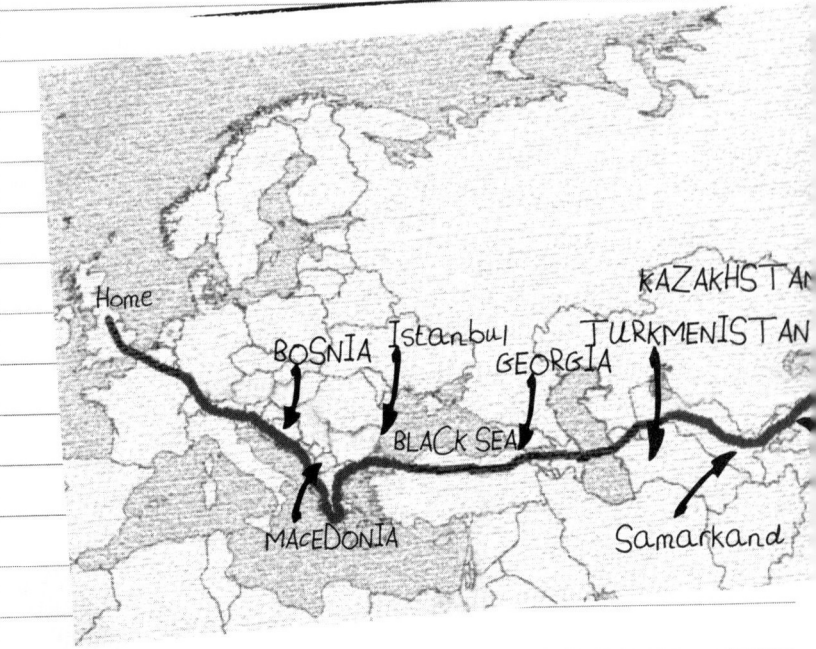

Punctures - MUST KNOW HOW to REPAIR!!

Punctures are annoying. But they are easy to mend and you're bound to get at least one on a bike adventure. So it's definitely worth learning how to fix one. You'll need:

- Two tyre levers
- A puncture repair kit
- A pump

Map to give you an idea of some of the places I went to!

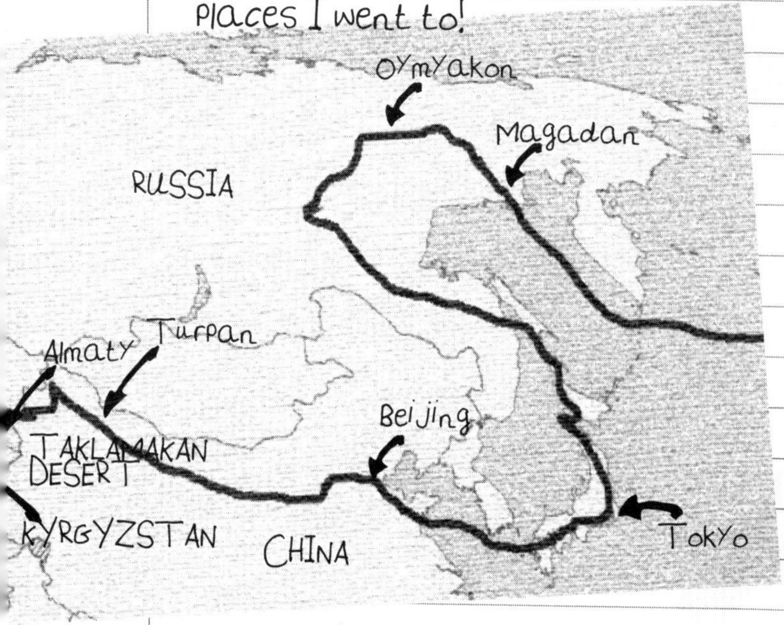

- Oymyakon
- Magadan
- RUSSIA
- Almaty
- Turpan
- TAKLAMAKAN DESERT
- KYRGYZSTAN
- Beijing
- CHINA
- Tokyo

Here's what to do:

1. Take off the wheel, then remove the tyre with your tyre levers.
2. Take out the punctured tube.
3. Pump up the tube, then listen for a hiss of air. If you can't find it, dunk it in water and look for the bubbles.
4. Clean and dry the tube. Pop a dollop of glue from the repair kit on the hole.
5. When the glue is nearly dry, stick on a patch and squeeze it tight.
6. Pop the tube back in the tyre, pump it up and re-attach the wheel. Carry on biking!

Half a World Away

Tom had been riding round the world for a long, long time now. Sometimes he thought back to the very beginning, back to his school classroom on a hot, sleepy afternoon. Back to the moment when he'd blurted out to everyone that he was going to cycle all the way round the planet. Even today, Tom was surprised he had actually said that out loud. He usually kept his daydreams to himself. Everyone had laughed, circling around him in the playground and telling him that he had no chance of succeeding.

Tom had blushed and felt a bit of a fool – he was just a boy daydreaming in a boring lesson at school. Cycling round the world was the sort of adventure people liked dreaming about, but not the sort of thing they would actually go on to do. It was too hard for a normal boy like Tom.

But once he'd spoken his dream out loud and the other boys and girls laughed at him, something inside Tom made him determined to give the trip a try. He didn't know if he could do it, but he would never find out if he didn't begin. It's exciting to try things when you don't know how they will turn out.

So Tom began.

He packed his camping kit, waved goodbye to his Mum, Dad and sister Lucy, and pedalled away down his street.

Step outside your house. Or look out of the window where you are reading this book right now. And just imagine for a minute ... If you cycled down that road you can see, turned left at the end, then turned right past the shops, up the hill, left at the traffic lights and just kept riding, you could get to anywhere on Earth. Anywhere at all! The street that you live on is the road to Siberia, or to Africa or to anywhere that you dream of.

Where do you dream of going when you are older? All of us dream of adventure, but not many act on those dreams. Tom was brave enough to get on his bike and go. And he just kept on going!

Tom rode across England. He cycled across Europe. Along the way he learned how to put up a tent, to fix a puncture, to read a map and to ask for directions in different languages. He didn't know much before he began, but he learned a lot along the way. Tom pedalled into Africa, marvelling at elephants and deserts and Maasai tribesmen.

Africa had been exciting, but it was just the beginning. Tom hitched a lift on a boat and sailed across the Atlantic Ocean. When he landed in South America a signpost showed it was 12,000 miles to Alaska. Tom climbed on his bike and started riding again. He rode over the colossal Andes mountains, sleeping in a tent and living off the cheapest food he could find. This was usually banana sandwiches (Tom's favourite food), though he did once eat a guinea pig, much to the annoyance of his sister Lucy who had a pet guinea pig!

Tom kept going – up through Mexico and into America, passing Hollywood with its movie stars and famous sign to arrive at a redwood tree so enormous that a car or a bike could pass through a hole in its trunk. Which he did immediately, of course. Can you imagine how big a tree needs to be for a car to be able to drive through it?

In Canada, forest fires blocked Tom's route and he was forced to build a raft and paddle for hundreds of miles down the Yukon River, through thick forests and past big, scary bears.

Reaching Alaska at last, Tom crossed the Pacific Ocean to Asia on a boat. Before he returned home again, back to his family and his comfy bed, he was going to ride thousands of miles through Russia, Japan, China and right the way across Asia and Europe.

Home was still half a world away.

Tom began this third and final leg of his journey in Magadan, on the shore of the Sea of Okhotsk, a tucked-away, little-visited corner of Russia. Magadan is the sort of town that Tom really loved; towns in the middle of nowhere, without tourists, towns he had never heard of and would probably never visit again.

He enjoyed seeing how normal people lived in normal little towns all over the world. In some ways their lives were just the same as his had been: going to school, helping with chores, playing with friends. But the details were different, and this was what made travel so interesting.

Tom met children in Africa who had to walk miles to collect water and carry it in buckets balanced on their heads. He met a boy in Peru who looked after his family's llamas. He met girls in California who went surfing before school. And now in Siberia, Tom met children whose school wouldn't give them a day off from lessons until the temperature dropped below -50°C!

Magadan looked like every other Russian town Tom would ride through. Old cars rattled down bumpy roads, crashing through potholes as their engines spluttered. Clouds of exhaust fumes billowed into the air. People lived in small flats above shops. The shops sold everything you could imagine – bread, sausages, balls of string. But they never had very much of any item so everything was spread out carefully on the shelves to make the shops look fuller.

Some Russians are very rich, but many are poor. Old ladies – known as *babushka* or "grandma" – sat on pavements trying to sell small piles of vegetables from their gardens, or jars of homemade jam, or a few eggs laid by their chickens.

"*Zdrastvoojte!*" they said to Tom.

"*Zdrastvoojte!*" smiled Tom. "Hello!"

Tom bought bread, jam, noodles and fat salami sausages.

THE BOY WHO BIKED THE WORLD

He was preparing for the wilderness ahead. To his disappointment, there were no bananas in any of the shops.

In Siberia, the land is frozen solid. Even in summertime the earth does not completely thaw. This is called permafrost. You cannot dig deep into permafrost to lay foundations, so buildings are built a little way off the ground on stilts. Water pipes and sewage pipes cannot be buried underground either, so they run overground, zig-zagging round street corners and crossing pavements. Sometimes on the pavement there is a stile to cross over the pipes, like when you climb into a field on a footpath.

The town of Magadan was built in 1930 by prisoners. They arrived in this empty area by ship, then were put to work chopping down trees and building a town. They built the only road that leads away from Magadan to reach the wealthy gold mines that are dotted across Siberia. This was the road that Tom was going to ride.

It was a cruel and harsh life back then, and Tom thought sadly of the prisoners as he cycled out of town and into the wild. A cold wind blew. Winter was on its way. Tom shivered and pedalled a little faster.

AMAZING FACTS ABOUT RUSSIA

Russia is the biggest country in the world, (70 times) bigger than Britain and twice as big as America. Russia is so big that when it is one time on one side of the country, it is <u>11</u> hours different on the other side! You could be having your breakfast in Russia whilst someone else thousands of miles away in Russia is tucked up and fast asleep in the middle of the night.

SIBERIAN TIGERS don't hibernate, but I'm unlikely to have to worry about them: today, there are fewer than 500 in the wild.

They can weigh up to 300kg and sadly nearly all of them have been killed for their beautiful fur. The same problem faces the AMUR LEOPARD: there are only around (45) still alive in the entire world. If we do not make massive efforts to save these beautiful big cats, they will soon be extinct.

The enormous shaggy Russian bears will be sleeping by now, thankfully. They hibernate throughout the long winter, curling up in cozy caves and sleeping for months on end! They live off the fat reserves in their bodies, so when they eventually wake up they are skinny and very hungry.

Lake Baikal in Siberia is 400 miles long, 50 miles wide and a mile deep. It is the world's largest freshwater lake and contains 20% of the world's non-frozen fresh water.

The Trans-Siberian train from Moscow to Vladivostok takes a week to complete its journey. It's the longest train journey in the world, running for nearly 6,000 miles. It has been running for 100 years.

Pancakes and Reindeer

After Magadan, there were no roadsigns. At times the road was only a dirt track. Often there was not any road at all. Sometimes the rivers were bridged, but often the bridges were uncared for and had collapsed.

On occasion, Tom could carefully tiptoe across a broken bridge and look down through big holes at the scary drop into the current below. But usually the only option was to take off his shoes and socks, roll up his trousers, and wade through the icy water, gasping at the cold and making a noise that sounded quite a lot like a monkey!

When this happened, his feet turned blue with cold. It was like an ice-cream brain freeze for his feet, but without the good bit of first enjoying the ice cream.

The temperature was low, but it was not yet viciously cold. Soon though, the temperature was going to plummet and even the rivers would freeze solid.

Winter arrived silently in the night. Big flakes of snow, millions of them, covered Tom's little tent and all of Siberia in a thick white blanket. Trees sagged under the weight. Animals shivered and settled down to hibernate through the long cold months; most of them would sleep until summer returned. Tom shook the snow from his tent, clambered out into the freezing morning air, and looked around. Amongst the vast white emptiness, he was the only moving thing.

Tom grinned. He loved snow! It was fun to play in. Back home snow might mean that school was cancelled, and those rare days were the best days ever. Now, here in Siberia, the snowflakes were still falling and would not stop falling for many days to come. Tom had never seen so much snow.

"Woohoo!" he shouted into the white, flakey sky.

But his voice sounded thin and small. There was nobody around to reply. No-one to throw a snowball at. And a nervous feeling started to grow inside Tom's tummy. Snow might look pretty. It might be fun back home. But cycling through Siberia in the middle of winter was going to be very hard indeed …

As soon as he began riding, Tom skidded and crashed. Cycling in snow is difficult! Tom gradually got the hang of it, but he still had to stop and push his bike whenever the snow was too deep to pedal through.

In a funny way it actually reminded him of crossing the boiling hot desert in Sudan, when he had to drag his bike through drifts of sand. Sand and snow aren't that different to a world cyclist like Tom.

Luckily, about once a day, a skidoo or a jeep passed Tom on the road. The jeeps' wheels packed the snow down, making a track that he could cycle along.

THE BOY WHO BIKED THE WORLD

One day a growling, roaring noise made Tom turn around. A tank was driving towards him, its caterpillar tracks easily gripping the snow. The roads in Siberia were so rubbish that these road workers had bought an old Army tank to drive instead of their work van! Tom laughed and waved as it passed.

The track was meandering backwards and forwards through the forest. The tank driver, though, decided to take a more direct route. He turned off the road and drove into the forest. The tank smashed the trees out of its way as it battered a new, straighter route. Tom was fed up with dragging his bike through the rutted, frozen marshland, so he was happy to follow the tank's shortcut through the destroyed section of forest. Anything that made the day less difficult was good. And following a tank through a Siberian forest was fun!

For miles, Tom cycled through the dark forest. There was no-one to talk to and he had only the trees for company. Finally, after several days he saw another vehicle. This one swooshed quietly across the frozen ground. Tom heard the hiss of metal runners, the panting of running animals. And then he heard the jingle of bells. It was a reindeer sleigh!

A tall man stood on the sleigh, holding the reins in thick gloves. He was wrapped from head to foot in fur. The reindeer steamed as they ran, their broad feet acting like snowshoes and gripping the snow. When the driver saw Tom he hauled on the reins and brought the sleigh slithering to a halt. In all his furs he looked more like a yeti than a man. But his big smile made Tom feel welcome.

The man had two gold teeth, and his narrow, dark eyes creased with laughter as he took in the sight of the boy on his bike. He had never seen a cyclist before. He was from the Yakut people who have lived in Siberia for a long, long time, hunting, fishing and herding reindeer. He spoke the Yakut language, so he and Tom had no way to speak to each other. But you can exchange lots of information without using words.

The man pointed to himself and said "Kaskil". That was his name. Tom pointed to himself and said "Tom".

Kaskil rubbed his tummy, showing that he was hungry.

Tom was always hungry so he did the same.

"Let's go and eat!" grinned Kaskil.

Kaskil picked up Tom's bike and placed it carefully onto the sleigh. Tom climbed up and stood beside the man, who shouted and cracked his whip. The reindeer galloped off at speed. Tom was so excited about riding on a reindeer sleigh that he didn't mind that they were zooming off in the direction that he had just ridden, nor that it was absolutely freezing.

After a short journey they arrived at a cluster of small homes deep in the forest. The houses were bungalows, built from long logs. In front of each home was a neatly chopped stack of firewood and an even bigger pile of ice blocks, about the size of pavement slabs. The ice had been cut from a river with long saws to provide water for the families.

Houses here did not have running water because it would freeze in the pipes. There were no flushing toilets for the same reason, so Kaskil's toilet was out in the back garden. It was little more than a hole in the ground inside a tiny shed – not a warm, cosy place to go to the loo! Tom once peered down into one of these holes and saw a big pyramid of frozen solid poo. Daily life can be tricky when you don't have sewers to carry your waste away!

But Kaskil's house was deliciously warm inside. Beside the log stove in the kitchen was a barrel of water, melted from the blocks of frozen ice outside. Kaskil pulled a chair close to the stove and motioned for Tom to sit down and warm up. He peeled off some of his enormous fur clothes.

Tom's new friend didn't have a fridge or a freezer. These aren't necessary when you can just keep your food on a shelf outside the back door. And besides, there was no electricity here to power them. Within minutes, a pan of delicious pancakes was sizzling away on the stove. Tom was very happy. He was warm. He'd ridden on a reindeer sleigh. And he was about to eat pancakes. Life was good!

Kaskil piled two plates high with pancakes. He heaped berries on top, berries he had gathered from the woods last autumn. On top of all this he blobbed a big pile of cream, made with milk from the cow in the barn next door. Tom and Kaskil could not speak the same language, but everyone knows the language of food. Grinning at each other, the two of them began to eat.

STAMP
REPUBLICA DE
PANAMA
ARGENTINA
SIBERIA
CANADA
FRANCE
CHILE
USA
PERU
TIKAL

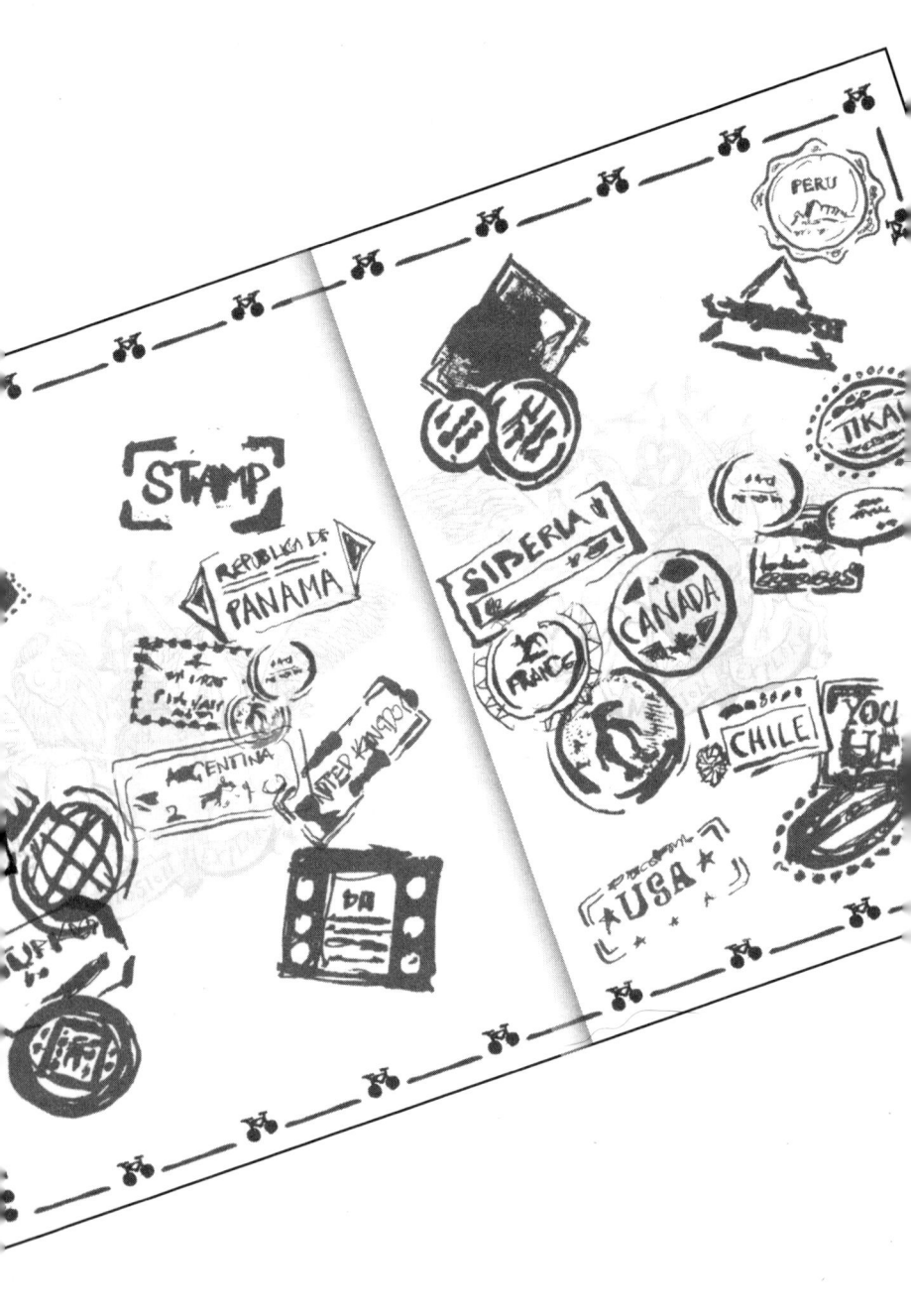

Riding the Wild Winter Road

Tom arrived at a branch in the road. He had a difficult decision to make. The left turn was called the Summer Road. The right fork was the Winter Road. Both roads ended up in the same place, but they could only be used for half the year each. The Summer Road took a high route through the hills. In winter it became blocked with snow. If Tom took that route and got stuck, nobody would pass by to help him for six months.

The Winter Road, on the other hand, stayed low, passing through swamps and across rivers with no bridges. It was impossible to travel that road until the weather was cold enough to freeze everything solid, including the rivers. One of these was the Lena River, the 11th biggest river in the world. It would need to become very cold indeed before the Lena River froze …

Tom was afraid. Making choices in the wilderness is difficult. There is nobody to help you make a decision. And if you make the wrong one, the consequences can be very, very serious.

It was almost evening and he was tired. He decided not to make his mind up immediately, but set up his tent at the junction to think about it. What road would you take?

Tom's tent was his home. It was a very small home, but it was all he needed as he cycled round the world. The kitchen, bedroom and living room were all in one place. In fact, Tom's tent was almost better than his real house. He ate his tea straight out of the pan whilst lying in bed (snuggled into his sleeping bag to keep warm). And he did the washing up in bed, too.

"Washing up" simply meant licking his spoon and pan clean. When he got home he was going to try to persuade his family to lick their plates rather than bothering to wash them up.

The only problem with living in a tent was the bathroom. If Tom needed the toilet he had to climb out of the tent into the freezing night air – definitely a job to do as fast as possible! Going to the toilet in the freezing cold was not fun, but Tom did enjoy cleaning his teeth outside, searching for shooting stars in the sky as he brushed.

Tom usually set an alarm to wake himself up in the morning, but if he was buried in a sleeping bag, he couldn't hear it. So in Siberia, he kept the alarm inside his woolly hat, near his ears, to make sure it woke him up.

But tonight, no alarm was necessary. Within an hour he woke up, shivering. Ice had built up on the inside of the tent and a thin layer covered his sleeping bag. Tom warmed himself up by wiggling his body as fast as he could. But all this activity made him wide awake. Finally, he fell asleep again, only to be woken up an hour later, cold and shivering once more. This went on and on.

Despite the disrupted sleep, by morning Tom had made his decision. He was going to ride the Winter Road. He did not want to risk being stranded for six months without seeing another person.

Getting up was the worst part of Tom's day. That was true at home too, when his Mum and Dad woke him from a lovely deep sleep and started shouting a thousand things to him at once.

"Get up! Get dressed! Eat your breakfast! Hurry Up! Clean your teeth! Are you still in bed?! Get up! Get dressed! Clean your breakfast! Eat your teeth! Hurry Up! You'd better not still be in bed …"

Mornings at home were annoying, noisy whirlwinds. But they were easy compared to mornings in Siberia. It's true Tom didn't have his parents shouting. He didn't have to go to school. He didn't even need to get dressed: here, Tom slept in his clothes at night. He'd given up changing his pants as he never took his clothes off. If he was cold, he used his spare pants for an extra hat!

But Tom *did* have to get out of his sleeping bag. And when the temperature outside was as cold as it is in Siberia, this was horrible! Tom forced his feet into frozen shoes, wishing he were back in his sleeping bag. He even wished he could go to school. At least school was warm.

Tom sprinted in circles round and round his tent like a daft dog chasing its tail. Then he did star jumps and whirled his arms like a windmill. Anything to get warm.

Each morning Tom spent an hour melting snow and pouring it into thermos flasks so he could drink it throughout the day. Finally, with numb fingers, he packed away his frozen, stiff tent and jumped on his bike to try to pedal a bit of warmth back into his body.

The temperature was -40° degrees Celsius.

Back home, when the weather gets to be about 5°C – as cold as a fridge – you'll hear people complaining and dreaming of summer. When the weather drops to freezing (0°C), fields turn crispy with frost and a skin of ice freezes across puddles.

Your freezer at home is about -20°C. Only really cold countries and high mountains regularly have temperatures that drop as low as -20°C. Hardly anywhere except the North Pole and the South Pole get down to -40°C.

And that's what the temperature was today. -40°C!

It's difficult to imagine just how cold -40°C is, except that it is colder than living inside your freezer. If you touch metal with bare skin your fingers stick to the metal. When you breathe out you can actually hear your breath freeze and tinkle to the ground. Men with beards get big build-ups of ice in them, and anyone with a runny nose grows disgusting snot icicles that dangle off the end of their nose.

If you take a cup of boiling water and throw it into the air at -40°C, the water turns into ice before it hits the ground.

THE BOY WHO BIKED THE WORLD

Once, one of Tom's beloved bananas froze so hard that he used it to hammer a nail into wood!

When you are somewhere really cold you must be sure to wear lots of loose layers of clothes. Layers make it easier to control your body temperature – you can take off a layer or put on another one. It's really important not to get too cold, of course. But it's equally important not to get too hot. Your sweat will later cool down and make you dangerously cold.

Omyakon is the coldest town in the world, with a record temperature of an astonishing -71°C. It was a small place, and some children had built an igloo in one of the gardens. As soon as Tom cycled into Omyakon, he dived into a café and bought some delicious hot pies. He was more excited about their warmth than their taste. He didn't want to waste any of that precious heat, so instead of putting the pies into his bags with his other supplies, he tucked them down inside his pants.

Not many people would want to eat pies that have been carried around inside their pants, but Tom was delighted to be able to enjoy them twice – once to warm himself up and once to savour their delicious taste!

Tom also bought some ice cream – one of his all-time favourite treats. Siberia was the only place in the world where Tom could carry ice cream around without it melting. Filling his bags (not his pants) with ice cream, he cycled onwards.

That night, wearing all his clothes and snuggled deep inside his sleeping bag, Tom licked an ice cream cone and smiled. He unzipped the tent door a little so that he could see the sky. The sky was filled with stars. Sweeping through and amongst the stars were the Northern Lights – swirling waves and curtains of magical-looking green light. The Northern Lights were one of the best things that Tom had ever seen. To enjoy them whilst he ate an ice cream was the perfect ending to a hard, cold day on the road.

Cycling home from Siberia was tough work. When you're wearing three pairs of gloves even easy jobs like fixing punctures take ages to do. And when you're not fixing punctures, you're skidding and crashing into snowdrifts. But in spite of the difficulties, Tom was making steady progress along the Winter Road.

Only one thing was worrying him: the Lena River. If he could not cross the river then he could not carry on. His adventure would be over. There was no bridge and – at this time of year – no ferry. Tom desperately willed the weather to get even colder, so that the Lena would freeze. It was horrible, but it was his only hope. He rode nervously on.

The Lena was the widest river Tom had ever seen – hundreds of metres across. But as he arrived on its banks, the boy breathed a sigh of relief and smiled. His sigh ballooned into a cloud in front of his mouth and fell as ice crystals to the ground. The river was frozen!

Cars were driving across the river. Just imagine how solid a river has to be before it can hold the weight of a car ...

Tom cycled out onto the Lena. Being on a frozen river is one of the most dangerous things you can ever do. Occasional gaps appeared in the ice as Tom inched forward. Filled with fear, he looked down at the cold black water racing beneath his feet. If he fell into that water he would certainly die. Tom was very careful to cross only on the patches of ice where the cars had been driving. This proved that the ice would be frozen enough for him and his bike.

With another big sigh of relief, he reached the other side. He had crossed the last big obstacle in Siberia. With as much speed as he could manage, he rode onwards. Siberia was wonderful, but Tom was beginning to dream of somewhere less painful, less frightening, less dangerous, and less cold.

Tom didn't have far to go and soon arrived at the coast, where he could catch a boat across the sea to his next country: Japan.

HOW TO BUILD AN IGLOO

Building an igloo warms you twice - once when you build it and once when you sleep in it!

Snow must be firm and stick together well. Using a snow saw (like a long bread knife), cut about 100 ice bricks - as long and wide as you can - about 25cm thick. Build a circular wall from the bricks. The circle must be big enough to sleep inside, but don't make it too big, as building an igloo is a lot of work!

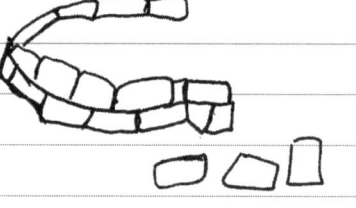

Saw a sloping angle from the top of the wall so that it begins low, but gets higher as you move round the circle. This helps give the spiral shape you want. Build another layer of the wall on top of the first layer. Pat the bricks down well to make sure they stick, and slope them slightly inwards. Keep building up the spiral wall, getting higher and closer to the middle.

Once the walls are nearly finished, cut one more block of snow and trim it carefully so that it sits in the hole at the top of the igloo, holding it all together.

I couldn't really draw this, so I put this picture in instead.

Finally, carve a tiny door. You might want to build an entrance tunnel to keep out the wind and drifting snow.

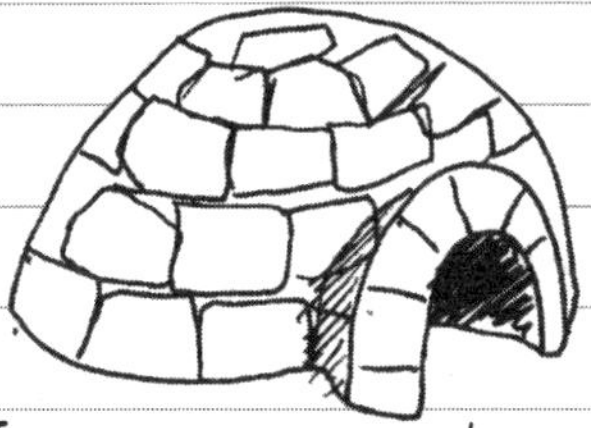

Once inside, replace the block of snow to keep out the cold.

Igloos are much warmer than you might imagine, and glow with a beautiful ice-blue light.

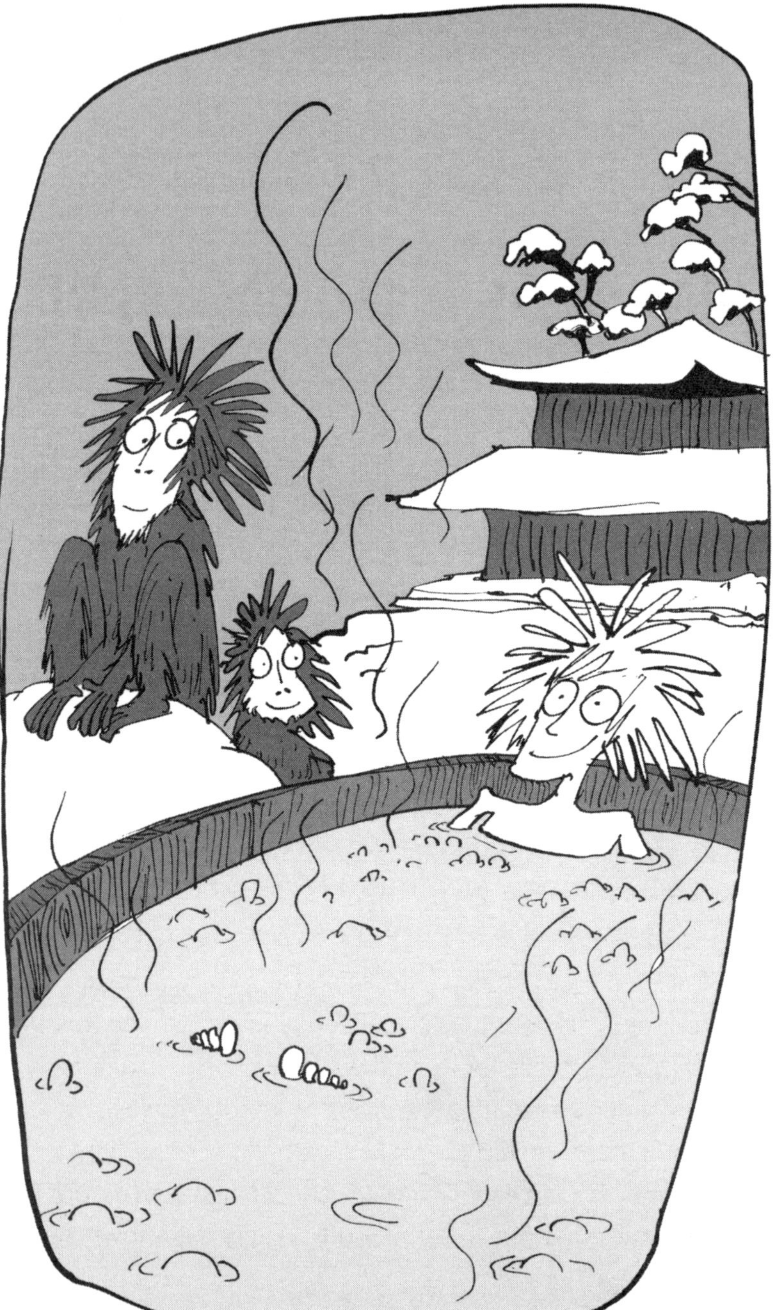

Steaming through Japan

Japan was different in every way to Russia. The people and shops looked different. The streets were busy with small, shiny cars. The signs were in Japanese, writing that Tom could not read. Everywhere he looked he saw traffic lights and flashing neon lights. He had not seen a traffic light in the last 3,000 miles of Siberia.

Because Tom normally cycled slowly from one country to the next one, he usually noticed that many things were the same in the two countries, rather than how different things were. There was little culture shock. But crossing a sea to a new country meant that the differences were greater. And he had never crossed between two countries as different from each other as Russia and Japan. The surprise and novelty were brilliant.

But Tom had a problem. He stank. He knew that he did – he could smell himself! It had not been enjoyable in the Russian cold to take off his clothes and wash in a river. He'd done it a couple of times but after the rivers froze solid it wasn't really Tom's fault that he couldn't take a bath. So now he stank!

His first job in Japan was to get clean. Japan is one of the cleanest countries in the world. Every little town has a public bath, an *onsen*, where you can go to wash and relax in a deep, hot tub. Tom was looking forward to this.

The *onsen* Tom cycled to was outdoors. Even though there was still snow on the ground, the water bubbling up from a natural hot spring was steaming hot. It was wonderful. Imagine how great it would feel to sit back and wallow in a hot outdoor bath on a cold, icy day.

There is a place in Japan where the local monkeys do exactly this. The red-faced monkeys relax in the steaming water, escaping from the cold snowy land that they live in.

Tom peered out from his big wooden bath and looked out over the wooded river valley. You might have mistaken Tom for a little monkey if you'd seen him grinning away in the hot water, red-faced, scruffy-haired and very happy to have put the cruel Siberian winter behind him.

Smelling good at last, Tom was ready now to cycle the whole way down Japan. Japan is made up of an incredible 6,852 islands, but nearly everyone lives on four main islands. These are called Hokkaido, Honshu, Kyushu and Shikoku.

Hokkaido is the northern island where Tom landed from Russia. Snow lay thick on the ground. Tom was fed up with snow. He was looking forward to the warmer islands further south. The Japanese word for snow is *yuki*. And after months of the stuff, that was pretty much how Tom was feeling about snow, too.

As he rode south, Tom cycled into springtime. He was delighted to see green fields again after endless fields of white. The first flowers of springtime smelled beautiful, and the blue sky and bright sunshine warmed his spirit.

THE BOY WHO BIKED THE WORLD

Cherry trees were bursting with pink blossom, like giant clouds of candy floss. Japanese people love the cherry blossom season because it welcomes in the spring and signals the end of winter. Spring is a time for new beginnings, a time for looking forward.

Tom was also looking forward to a banana sandwich. He had missed bananas. There were plenty available here so he bought a bunch and settled beneath a cherry tree to make a huge sandwich, drooling at the thought.

As he chomped away happily, an old man approached Tom. He had a long moustache and carried a travel-worn satchel.

"*Konnichiwa!*" said the old man, bowing. "Hello!"

"*Konnichiwa!*" replied Tom, bowing back.

The old man sat down next to Tom under the cherry tree.

"My name is Tom," said Tom, pointing to himself to explain.

"Matsuo," said the man. He touched himself on the nose as he spoke – this is what Japanese people do when they talk about themselves. It looks quite funny.

Tom offered Matsuo a sandwich. Japanese people are very polite, but even though he said "no thank you", Tom could tell that Matsuo thought a banana sandwich was a bit disgusting.

They chatted about Tom's adventure until he finished eating. As Tom packed up his things and got ready to ride again, Matsuo wrote him a little poem. Short poems like this, called *haiku*, are popular in Japan:

On a journey,
Resting beneath the cherry blossoms,
I feel myself to be in an old play.

JAPANESE FOOD - YUMMY!

Some things I ate in Japan were:

- Yakitori - barbecued chicken on skewers
- Onigiri - the alternative to a sandwich. A rice ball with something like tuna in the middle, wrapped in a shiny layer of seaweed like tissue paper
- Okonomiyaki - something between an omelette and a pancake
- Takoyaki - fried balls of octopus. Really tasty, even if you don't think you'll like it!
- Ramen - noodle soup. The louder you slurp it, the better it tastes!
- Tempura - battered and fried vegetables dipped in soy sauce
- Gyoza - Dumplings filled with pork and fried. Dip in soy sauce and eat steaming hot.

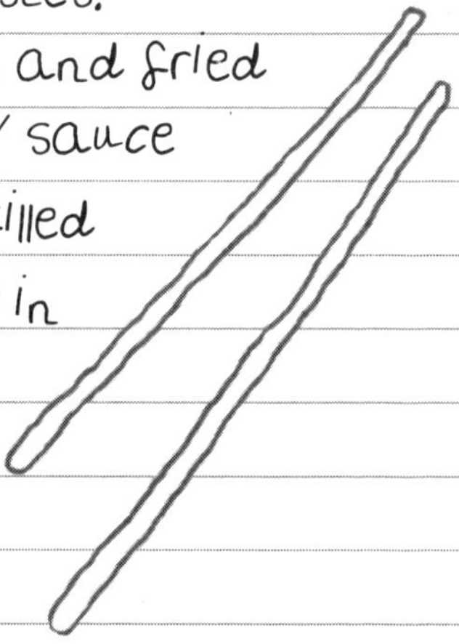

Oishi! Delicious!

JAPANESE BOWING

Japanese people are extremely polite and I've had to learn lots of new things. Like bowing.

When you bow "hello" you bend a short way while looking at the ground.

Matsuo's pic of me bowing!

Boys bow with their hands at their side.
Girls bow holding their hands.

When somebody bows to you, it is polite to bow back. Sometimes, though, the person will then bow back at you again and so you also have to bow back at them. This can carry on for a long time!

When you apologise, you bow several times. The more trouble you are in and the more you want to say "sorry", the deeper you bow.

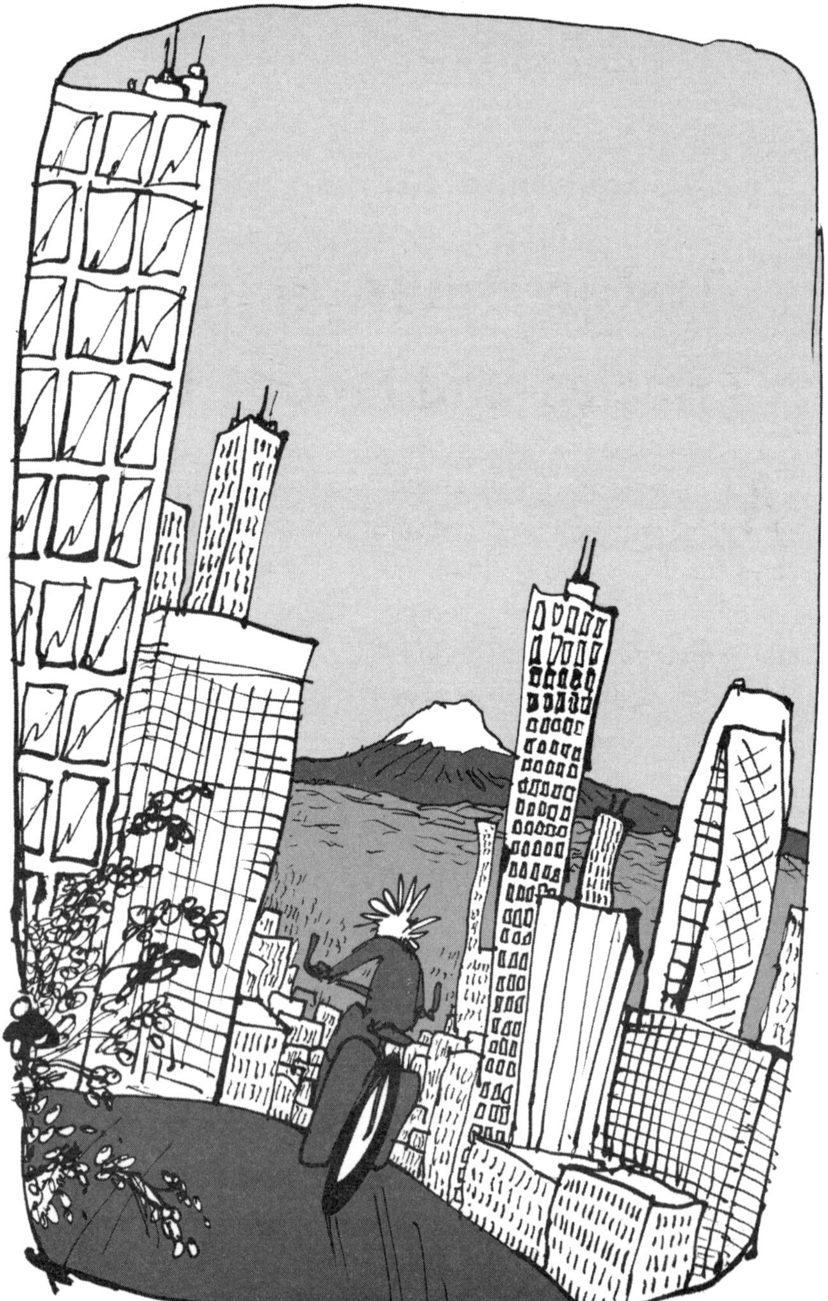

Tokyo Tower Blocks, Temples and Mount Fuji

A few years ago Tom had been friends with a Japanese boy at school. Michitaka had since returned to live in Japan, and emailed Tom to invite him to visit his family in Tokyo.

Tokyo is one of the biggest cities in the world. It is about three times bigger than London. It took a whole day for Tom to cycle into the city. He grew annoyed with the hundreds of traffic lights that kept interrupting him. Every time the traffic stopped, thousands of people swarmed across the road.

As he approached the centre of Tokyo, the buildings towered higher and higher above Tom's head, blotting out the sky. Restaurant signs flashed brightly with words he could not understand. Luckily, many Japanese restaurants have plastic models of their meals as well as menus, so when he stopped to eat Tom could just point to a model that looked particularly tasty.

After the emptiness of Siberia it was weird to be surrounded by all these man-made things. Tom felt excited but a bit overwhelmed as he rode through Tokyo. Trying to weave through the busy city streets using a street map with

Japanese writing was very difficult. He was looking forward to seeing his friend again; Tom only ever met strangers on his journey. This sometimes felt a bit lonely. He was both surprised and pleased with himself when he eventually made it to Michitaka's address. He rang the bell.

"Hi, Tom!" said Michitaka , opening the door.

"Hi, Mitch!"

"Come in!" Michitaka said, smiling. "You stink!"

It was good to see his friend again.

Tom loved staying with Mitch and his family. And also wearing freshly washed clothes. They played computer games and watched football on TV, just like they used to. It was interesting to see what was different in Mitch's home in Japan compared to Tom's in England. Tokyo is very crowded so almost everyone lives in tiny flats.

Mitch showed Tom around. "In Japan, you must always take your shoes off when you come inside. When you go into the bathroom, you have to put on these special toilet slippers. Remember to take them off again when you come out or everyone will think you're gross!"

In the bathroom, Mitch pointed at the toilet. He grinned.

"Japan's toilets are the best in the world. You'll like this …"

He pressed a button on the toilet and music began to play.

"It's got a heated seat, too!"

Tom thought of Kaskil's freezing outdoor toilet in the forest in Siberia.

"I love heated toilets!" he said.

The Boy Who Biked the World

Mitch's Mum and Dad, Miyako and Katsumi, did not speak English so Mitch translated their chat. Tom was learning to eat with chopsticks and usually made a terrible mess. One morning, Miyako cooked a fried egg for Tom's breakfast. Eating a fried egg with chopsticks was a complete disaster! The next day, Miyako gave Tom a small present. Everyone laughed as Tom opened a packet containing training chopsticks that Japanese babies use when they are first learning how to hold chopsticks.

At mealtimes, Mitch's family knelt on the floor around a low table. Japanese food was different to any food Tom had eaten before. It always looked beautiful, served in tiny portions on small plates. Slurping things like noodle soup meant that you were enjoying the food and, in Japan, is not a rude sound.

It was impossible, though, to guess what different foods were going to taste like until you popped them into your mouth. Some things were sweeter than they looked. Others were chewy. Or slimy. Some were delicious. And some were disgusting!

Mitch found it hilarious to wait until Tom had swallowed something before telling him what he had just eaten. "Jellyfish tentacles! Rotten beans! Raw squid in liver sauce! Chicken neck!"

If you're going to travel round the world you need to get brave at trying different foods. Tom was an expert by now, so he even managed to swallow the jellyfish tentacles with a smile.

Every time he ate something disgusting Tom said *"oishi!"* *Oishi* means delicious. It made the chef happy when Tom said it, so he said *oishi* a lot, even when things were not very *oishi* at all.

———🚲———

It had been wonderful visiting Mitch, but soon it was time for Tom to hit the road. Bidding the family a heartfelt "thank you", he climbed back on his bike and pedalled out onto the swarming streets of Tokyo. Cycling carefully but as fast as he dared, it was a relief to reach the countryside again.

Up ahead, Tom spotted the famous outline of Mount Fuji. Mount Fuji is a volcano, but it hasn't erupted for 300 years, so its top is covered with a perfect cone of snow. Mount Fuji is the highest spot in Japan and you can see it from a long, long way away.

Cycling was much easier when the sun was shining and the road was free from snow. Tom zoomed along, making speedy progress. He rode down past the cities of Hiroshima and Nagasaki and on towards the south of the country.

Between the busy towns, Tom passed peaceful temples, half-hidden on hilltops amongst the trees. There are thousands of temples in Japan. One of the most fantastic is called Kiyomizu-dera. It is a massive wooden structure built almost 400 years ago without using a single nail.

The main hall is surrounded by cherry blossom trees. Beneath the temple's curved roofs is a broad balcony looking out over a beautiful forest. In olden days people believed that if they jumped from the veranda and didn't die, then their wishes would come true. As Tom peered cautiously over the edge he was glad that people didn't try this anymore: it was higher than the roof of his house!

Tom's favourite area of Japan was Shikoku island. It was wilder and less crowded than other parts of the country. The mountainous Iya Valley twists and turns, following the route of the rivers that carved out the steep slopes. Bridges made from vines are the only way to cross the river. High on a cliff-edge above the valley is a statue of a young boy peeing off the cliff down into the depths of the valley below!

Tom pedalled through leafy wooded valleys, then through groves of orange trees and on down the Pacific coastline. The cycling was fun and easy. He weaved in and out of rocky bays with clear green water and neat white fishing boats. At night he camped amongst the dunes, enjoying the luxury of not nearly freezing to death in his tent.

In the morning, Tom looked out of his tent at the sun rising over the Pacific Ocean. Japan is often known as the Land of the Rising Sun, and its flag has a picture of a rising sun. Somewhere far across that ocean lay California and the many beaches that Tom had camped on as he cycled up the coast of America.

After almost two years following the coast of the Pacific Ocean, it was time at last for Tom to say goodbye – *sayonara* – to the world's biggest ocean. It was time to ride across China.

SUMO!!

Yesterday Mitch took me to watch a sumo wrestling match. It was so exciting and funny. Thousands of cheering people packed into the stadium.

Down in the ring two gigantic wrestlers prepared for battle. I couldn't believe how big they were. The heaviest-ever sumo wrestler weighed 287kg. He ate 10 times more each day than normal grown-ups. If you want to get as fat as a sumo wrestler, you have to eat tonnes of food and not ride your bike at all.

The aim of sumo is to throw the other wrestler to the ground or out of the ring. That's why the wrestlers are massive! They wear just a loin cloth, like a pair of pants, which is pretty funny. They try to get hold of each other's pants, lift the other fighter and smash them to the ground.

Beforehand, they stamp around trying to scare each other. They scowl, lift their legs high, and throw handfuls of salt in the air. These attempts to look scary usually take longer than the fight itself! The fight begins when both wrestlers put their fists on the ground at the same time.

Suddenly they explode into action, smashing forwards into each other. It's amazing! The fights are over in just a few seconds as one of them is hurled to the ground with a massive crash.

Watching the sumo was hilarious, but it was also impressive to see how fast and strong the wrestlers are.

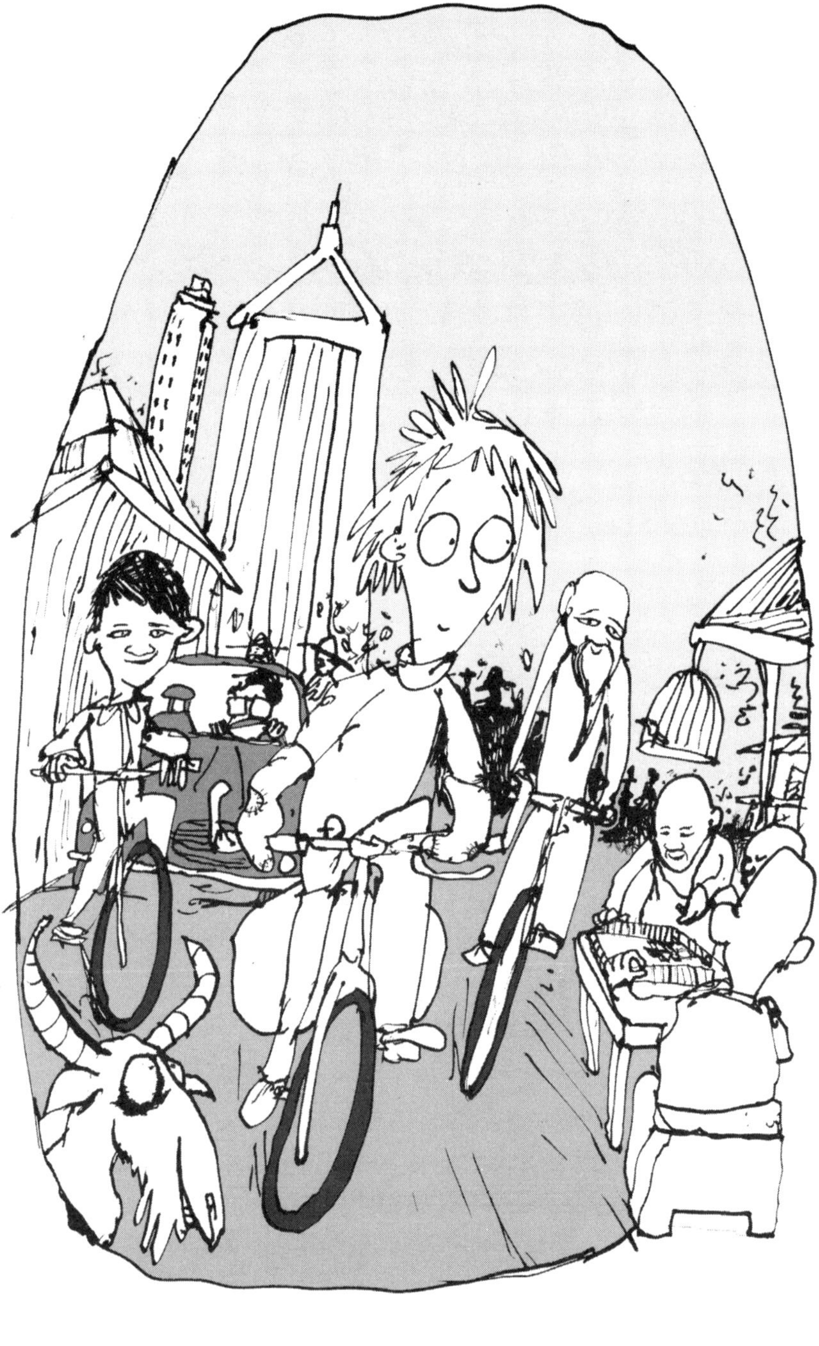

Chaos and Chopsticks in China

The noise hit Tom first. Japan had been quiet and orderly. China was noisy and chaotic. In the streets, crowds of people pushed past each other, laughing, shouting and jostling.

Qingdao, the city where Tom arrived by boat, had shiny skyscrapers just like Tokyo. But away from the city centre the roads were potholed and busy and rubbish blew in the wind. Battered cars beeped their horns and swerved crazily through the traffic. None of this happened in clean, organised Japan.

Tom rode past street stalls – little shacks selling sizzling food cooked on homemade charcoal stoves. The delicious smells of food mingled with the dirty fumes and the stink of sewers.

Tom's senses were on overload, and inside he was bubbling with excitement. His favourite thing in the whole world was to arrive somewhere new, somewhere surprising, and head out in search of adventure. He knew little about China, but he was excited to learn and explore.

It was much colder in Qingdao than in the south of Japan. Tom wrapped up as warm as he could, pulling his spare pair of socks over the top of his gloves. He pedalled into the countryside. Riding through villages, Tom dodged the goats that strolled around the road as they happily ignored the beeping cars. Passing homes, he glanced through doorways, spotting paper lanterns and hearing the gentle chirruping from songbirds or crickets kept as pets in little cages.

Old men sat round low tables playing *mahjong*, a game a bit like dominoes. The tiles are slammed down as noisily as possible. Tom waved at a cluster of boys, squatting in a circle playing marbles. He was too cold to stop and join in, though, and too excited.

Here he was, on the edge of the third biggest country in the world, surrounded by a billion people who – as yet – he couldn't say a single word to. He couldn't read the roadsigns either, which was a problem when he had thousands of miles to cycle through China. Nobody knew Tom. Nobody knew that he was here. And all these things made Tom very happy indeed. It was new; it was unknown; it was difficult. It was perfect!

Tom always enjoyed sharing the road with other cyclists and there were millions of them in China. All the bikes in China were the same – black and heavy. The men riding them wore matching blue flat caps. Ladies wore masks over their noses and mouths to protect them from China's disgusting, polluted air. It was the worst that Tom had come across on his ride around the world.

THE BOY WHO BIKED THE WORLD

Some bikes were clunky three-wheelers, piled high with stuff to be sold at market. Tied to the bikes were shiny piles of pots and pans that clanked, baskets of chickens (that clucked), and bundles of mops and buckets. One bike even had a pair of grumpy-looking pigs strapped to it!

Everyone stared at Tom as he pedalled past. He looked very different to the Chinese villagers. They were not used to seeing foreigners, and people in China are definitely not shy about staring.

Tom smiled and waved. They waved back and called out, "*Ni hao!*"

"*Ni hao … Ni hao …* Hello!" Tom practised saying to himself. He'd just learned his first Chinese word.

Tom had become good at using sign language when he couldn't speak the language – clucking like a hen when he wanted eggs, putting his hands together at the side of his head and closing his eyes when he wanted to sleep, rubbing his tummy when he was hungry and so on. Bit by bit he managed to communicate with the people he met, despite having no common language.

Spoken words were one thing, but making any sense of Chinese writing was quite another matter. As in Japan, Tom could not read or write a single word. But China was harder than Japan for Tom to travel through because, away from the big cities, hardly anyone in China understood the Latin alphabet Tom knew. This made things very complicated. For example, one day Tom bought a carton of milk. He was very thirsty. He opened it and took a massive gulp. Instantly he spat it out, all over the road – he had actually bought soy sauce, not milk.

Luckily, Tom found some help. He met a teacher who spoke English. Seow Hong helped Tom prepare some cards with Chinese writing on them. When he needed something, he could show the cards, which was very helpful. The cards had phrases in both Chinese and English such as:

- "I am really hungry. Please can I buy a big plate of food?"
- "Is there somewhere nearby where I can camp for the night?"
- "How far is it to the next place where I can get food and water?"
- "My name is Tom, I come from England, and I am cycling round the world."

What other phrases do you think would be useful for Tom? When Tom showed his cards to people they smiled and gave him the thumbs-up sign, a sign that seems to be understood all over the world. Then they would try to help. China was very noisy and the people did really disgusting spits all the time, even when they were cooking meals. But everyone was generous and friendly.

The young cyclist had one more handy trick to help him communicate. A Chinese journalist interviewed Tom about his adventures in the 50 countries he had pedalled across so far. They had chatted in English and then the journalist translated the story into Chinese. When the article was printed in the newspaper, there was a big photo of Tom and his bike at the top of the page.

Tom cut the article out of the newspaper. He had no idea what the reporter had written, but every time he showed the story to someone, the person read it carefully and then clapped Tom on the back as if to say "well done". Then they laughed a lot and gave him a big plate of food for free! This was good news, as Tom really loved Chinese food. Especially noodles.

To make noodles, a chef creates dough and stretches it out as far as his arms can reach. Then he brings his hands together so that he has a big loop of dough. Taking both ends of the loop in one hand, with the other hand he holds the loop in the middle so that he now has two fat strands of dough. The chef does this over and over again. Each time, the number of strands of dough double in number. They also get thinner. In just seconds a big piece of dough has changed into 2, 4, 8, 16, 32, 64, 128 strands of noodle. Tom, the hungry cyclist, drooled as he watched. 128 noodles was a feast!

The chef chucked the noodles into a pan of boiling water. As they bubbled away, he grabbed a big wok and threw in handfuls of chopped vegetables, chicken and tofu, followed by herbs and spices. Stirring the food as it sizzled furiously, the chef had Tom's lunch ready in just two minutes!

As he pedalled through the country, though, Tom learned that not all Chinese food is so delicious, not like the takeaway back home. One time he went to a night market that sold all sorts of weird food: fried scorpions, seahorses, snake, centipede. It was then that he really, really wished he had a banana sandwich!

Another time, after he'd finished a meal, Tom learned that he had just eaten dog! This is quite normal in parts of China, but Tom's sister Lucy would be very cross if she ever found out. He didn't think he wanted to eat dog again but had to admit it didn't taste too bad.

Tom found it hard to describe what dog tastes like. The best way he could explain it was that it tasted a bit like cat ...

After so much practice in Japan, Tom imagined himself to be a bit of an expert when it came to using chopsticks. But the Chinese people he met seemed to disagree. Many of the cafés Tom ate in were nothing more than a few stools clustered beside the road. So crowds of people gathered to stare wherever he ate. Traffic jams even developed as cars slowed down to take a look. These were the biggest crowds Tom had attracted since he had ridden through Ethiopia in Africa.

When Tom ate with chopsticks, everyone roared with laughter. And if a noodle should slip from his grasp, this was the funniest thing of all. Cycling round the world had taught Tom not to be shy and he was quite used to people laughing and being surprised at the things he did.

Every country in the world does normal things a little bit differently. In Japan, people touch their noses when talking about themselves; in Bulgaria they nod their heads when they mean "no". And different cultures have many different styles of eating, from knife and fork, to hands, to chopsticks.

As the crowds chuckled, Tom quietly ate his meal, often studying a map at the same time to work out how much further he had to ride that day. But one lunchtime, he spotted a joker in the crowd. The man was making everyone laugh by miming the way that in Tom's country people ate with a knife and fork, rather than with chopsticks: slice, spike, eat. Slice, spike, eat.

Everyone was laughing. But the biggest laugh of all came when Tom pointed out to the joker that he was holding his imaginary knife and fork in the wrong hands. The joker was actually doing worse with his cutlery than Tom was doing with his chopsticks. At least Tom had them in the proper hand, even if a few noodles did fall on the floor every meal!

Chinese people also enjoyed the way Tom wrote. It seemed strange to them. When he finished lunch, he always spent a few minutes writing his diary or a postcard home. People clustered around to have a look, peering over his shoulders as he wrote. They had no idea what Tom was writing.

Sometimes the people staring at Tom crowded in a bit too close. This was annoying. He never had any peace and quiet in China. So because he knew that nobody could read English, Tom sometimes amused himself by writing things like "this old man staring at me has got a really big nose".

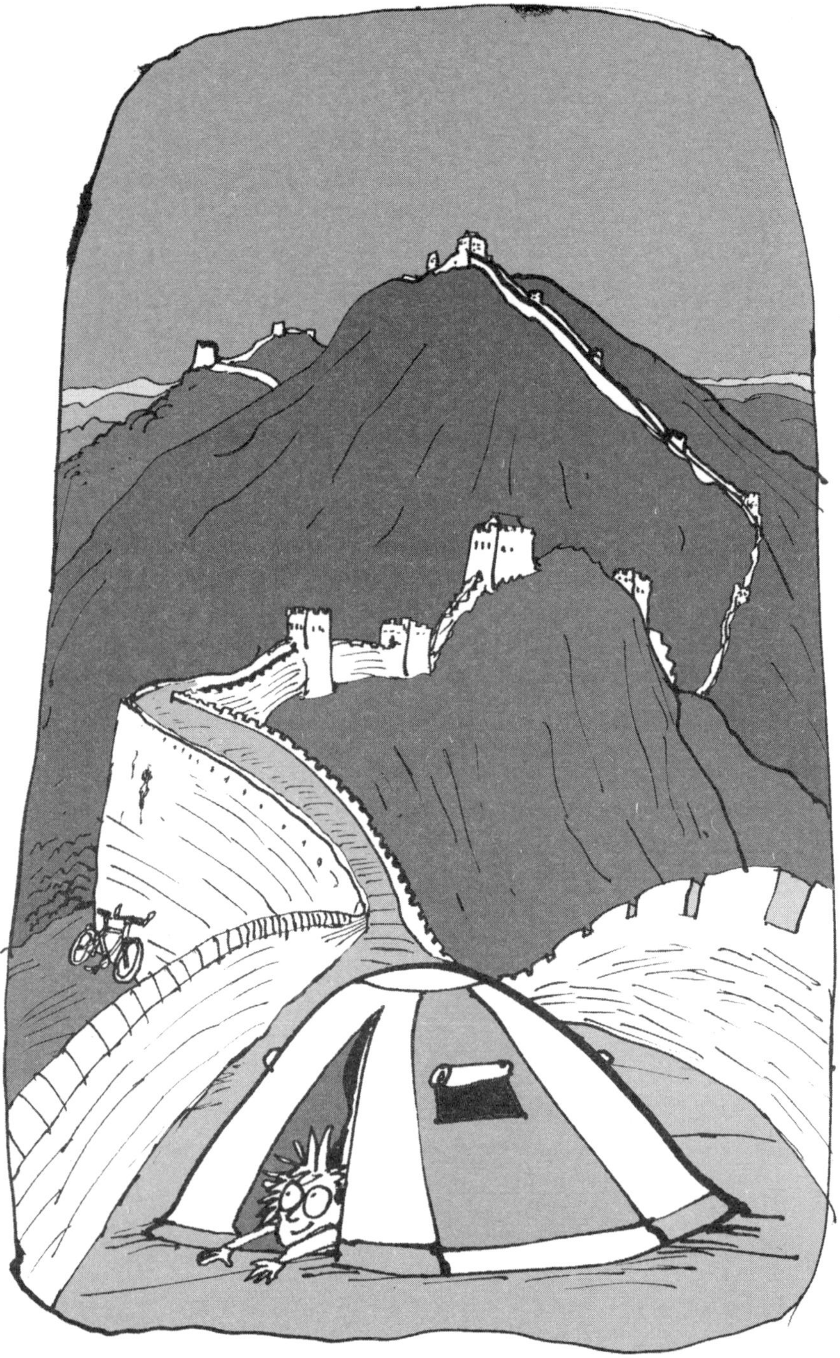

Beijing to the Great Wall

China's capital city, Beijing, was totally different to the small villages that Tom had been pedalling through. Beijing is the bit of China that the rest of the world usually sees, and so the streets are kept spotlessly clean. Shiny skyscrapers soar up into the murky sky. But there is so much pollution in Beijing that in the mornings Tom's eyes stung. The sunrises are pale lemon-yellow, and quite beautiful through the disgusting thick air.

Higher only than the skyscrapers are the hundreds of kites that fluttered in the sky as Tom rode past. Children in Beijing love flying kites. The kites are often decorated with birds, dragons or scary faces.

Riding into big cities was usually the worst part of Tom's trip because of all the traffic. But cycling into Beijing was fantastic fun. At rush hour the wide cycle lanes are filled with millions of cyclists, all sweeping along into the city together. It was great to ride in such huge crowds and was also much safer than dodging traffic by himself.

Just as Tom arrived in Tiananmen Square, he felt his tyre go flat. A puncture. Getting a puncture is always a bit annoying, but getting a puncture in one of the most famous city squares in the world was better than usual. In such a crowded city, the world's fourth biggest square was so big it felt as empty as being out at sea.

Tom sat down by the gate to the Forbidden City to fix his wheel. The Forbidden City was once the greatest palace in China.

You might think that Chinese people would be used to seeing someone fix a puncture as they have so many bikes themselves. But they were definitely not used to seeing a boy like Tom, a boy who was cycling round the world. And so of course a crowd gathered, staring and talking about Tom as he plucked out the nail that had caused the puncture.

Chinese police are very suspicious and don't like large gatherings; they worry that people might be getting up to mischief. Within minutes the police arrived. They wore big green hats, dark sunglasses and shouted very loudly until they discovered that the cause of the crowd was nothing more troublesome than a young boy fixing his bike.

In Beijing, the streets are busy with people in expensive clothes chatting on smartphones. There are American shops like McDonalds and Starbucks, and lots of expensive foreign cars. Every country in the world has rich people and poor people. But the difference in how people live was more striking in China than almost anywhere else Tom had cycled.

Just one day's ride away from Beijing's skyscrapers are villages where farmers plough tiny fields using ancient wooden ploughs. They live in mud-brick homes roofed with clods of earth. These people's lives have not changed in hundreds of years.

THE BOY WHO BIKED THE WORLD

China is becoming richer at an amazing speed, but there are still millions of very poor people. The country is developing fast. New cities are springing up all the time with big roads and super high-speed railway lines connecting them.

Tom cycled into a wide valley terraced with rice fields. Through the valley ran a broad river – China's famous Yellow River. It was a pale muddy colour, not exactly yellow. But Yellow River is a better name for one of the world's great rivers than Slightly Muddy River.

His heart sank. There was no bridge! Tom had ridden a quiet, empty road to get here as he liked looking for wilder routes away from main roads. But he had not expected the road to simply end. This was bad news. Maybe even BAD NEWS.

The road Tom was on was brand new, so it had been a bit of a puzzle as to why it was deserted. But now he understood why he hadn't seen any cars for days. He was on a road to nowhere.

Tom was stuck. He hated the thought of having to turn round and go all the way back. But there seemed to be no other choice. He could not cross the Yellow River. So Tom did what he always did when he had a problem: he sat down and ate a banana sandwich.

The sandwich cheered him up a bit, but he still couldn't think of a solution. He put off making a decision by fixing another sandwich. He couldn't risk using up his precious supply of bananas, so he made a bread sandwich instead.

Bread sandwiches don't taste very nice, but they are very cheap. Here's how to make a bread sandwich:
- Get a piece of bread
- Put another piece of bread on top of it (this is the sandwich's tasty filling)
- Put another piece of bread on top of that
- Squash it down and eat it

Tom's other trick for putting off making difficult decisions was to take a nap. So he rested his head on a rock that looked like a pillow even if it didn't feel like one, and drifted off to sleep to dream about bridges and bananas.

Some time later he woke to the sound of a spluttering engine. It sounded like one of the millions of smelly little motorbikes that zoom all around Asia. But for once this was not a motorbike. It was an engine on a barge. A barge, on the river. A barge heading his way.

Tom couldn't believe it. As quick as a flash he jumped to his feet. He leaped up and down and yelled as loudly as he could. Luckily the man steering the boat spotted him. With a surprised look, he turned the boat towards the riverbank and headed for the deranged, dirty boy who was jumping up and down.

The barge came gently alongside the riverbank. Tom was saved! The man on the barge beckoned for him and his bike to climb aboard. Tom didn't need asking twice. He didn't care where the barge was going so long as he didn't have to cycle back all the way he had just come.

The Boy Who Biked the World

With hand gestures and a bit of pointing, Tom managed to explain that he wanted to cross the Yellow River. The man smiled, turned the barge towards the opposite bank and puttered slowly across the river. The little engine was too weak for the big barge and the current was swift. So they drifted downstream as they crossed.

Soon the barge bumped gently onto the opposite bank. Tom jumped down onto the riverbank. He smiled and shouted "*xie xie*! Thank you!" The man waved goodbye and motored down the famous river.

The boy had no idea where the boat had come from, nor where it was going. He was always grateful but no longer surprised by the kindness of strangers on this adventure. It was weird how often funny little things like this happened to help him when he was stuck.

Tom scrambled up the muddy riverbank and heaved his bike up through the fields on the other side of the valley. It was exhausting work. By the time he reached the lip of the valley it was late afternoon. He was dripping with sweat and filthy with mud.

He was definitely not expecting the view that greeted him when he looked over the rim of the valley: a gigantic city, with huge power station chimneys belching black fumes into the sky.

The city was not on Tom's map. He had expected wilderness. This was a brand new city that had been built since his map was made. New cities like this, in the middle of nowhere, are springing up all over China. This explained the road that Tom had had all to himself: it was a road to this city. But the city was so new that the bridge to link the city with the road hadn't been built yet.

In the fields all around were roadsigns that showed junctions and roundabouts. They had not been built yet either, but the signs were already in place. Tom camped in a field next to a signpost for a roundabout. In a few months' time, this quiet field would be swallowed up by roads and buildings.

That night, to celebrate crossing the Yellow River, Tom ate both his remaining bananas. He could buy more food in the brand-new city.

Weeks later, Tom rode into a region of China known as Inner Mongolia. The land here is flat and empty. Far away across the plains Tom saw a shepherd with his flock of skinny sheep, his face wrapped in a scarf to protect him from the fierce, cold wind. The wind blew clouds of stinging dust into Tom's eyes as he struggled on, mile after mile, into the fierce headwind.

It was tough riding. But in the distance Tom spotted something that made him smile. He span the pedals as quickly as he could, although this wasn't very fast because of the wind. Nevertheless, Tom couldn't contain his excitement: it was the Great Wall of China.

THE BOY WHO BIKED THE WORLD

Reaching it at last, Tom leaned his bike up against the most famous wall in the world. He had arrived! At the Great Wall of China! Because the headwinds were driving him mad; because there was nobody for miles around; and because it seemed such a fun idea, Tom decided to stop riding early and sleep on top of the Great Wall of China!

It was a struggle to climb the wall, but well worth it. Tom pitched his tent on top of the Great Wall and grinned. This was one of the best campsites ever. He took a photo, just to make his family jealous.

As evening approached, the wind dropped and the air became still. Tom sat outside his tent, on top of the Great Wall, and looked around. The view was brilliant.

To the north, the rolling plains stretched off into the distance towards Mongolia. Far away in the west, where the sun was setting, was a tall range of snow-covered peaks – the Tien Shan mountains – that Tom still had to get across. Stretching away in front of him towards these mountains was a great desert, the Taklamakan Desert.

He blew up his inflatable globe. With his finger, Tom traced the route of the Great Wall of China. It was incredible that something man-made could stretch for such a distance.

The boy found where he was on the globe, then spun the globe in his fingers until he could see his home. Tom had a long way to go still, but in his travels he had come much further already. He smiled to himself, enjoying the sunset on top of the Great Wall.

GREAT WALL OF CHINA

The Great Wall of China is the largest man-made structure in the world. More than 10 million tourists visit the part near Beijing each year. It is a collection of walls, thousands of miles long, built bit by bit over many years.

The Great Wall looks like a dragon's back as it twists and winds its way across China, curving up and down mountain ranges and across mighty deserts. Work first began on the wall more than 2,000 years ago, and the Chinese even invented the wheelbarrow to help their work.

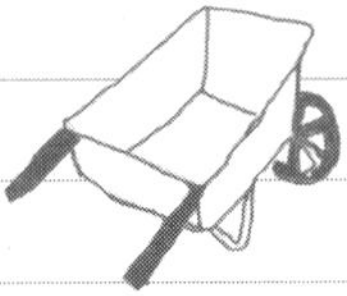

Over a million people, mostly soldiers and prisoners, built it over many centuries. The wall, and its thousands of forts, was built to defend China from invasions from Mongolia in the north. Soldiers in the forts used weapons such as hammers, spears, crossbows and the earliest forms of cannons to fight with. They could communicate across vast distances by using smoke signals and flags.

The Great Wall changes its look as it moves across China. In the east it is built from stones and bricks. The part of the wall near Beijing is the bit you usually see photos of. Further west, the wall passes through desert areas where there are no stones, so there it is built out of hard-packed mud.

COUNTING IN CHINESE ON ONE HAND

This was not only useful, but good fun. Try it yourself!

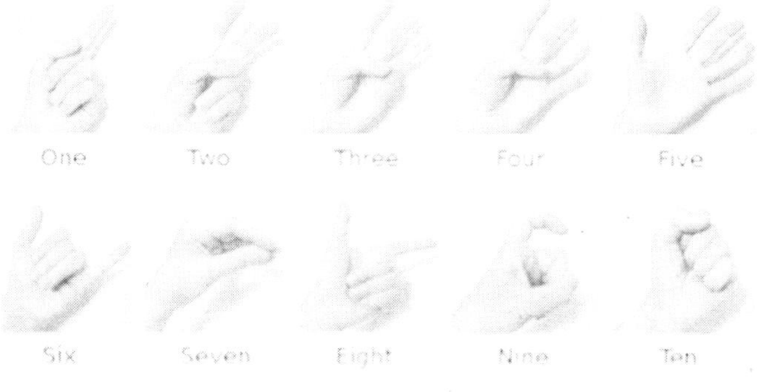

One	Two	Three	Four	Five
Six	Seven	Eight	Nine	Ten

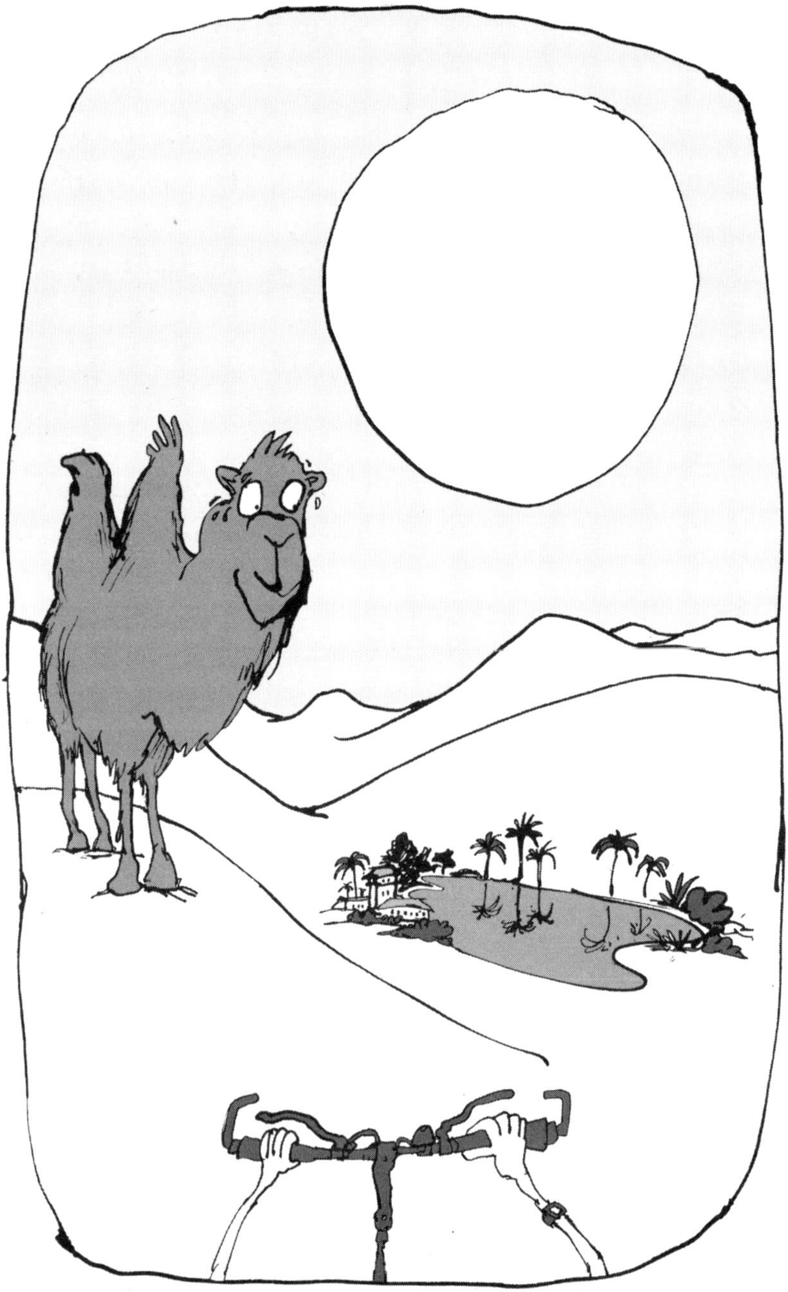

The Taklamakan Desert

Tom first spied the desert from the top of the Great Wall of China. In olden times, the next stage of his journey would have been fearsomely difficult. In the local language the word "Taklamakan" means "the person who goes into this desert will not get out the other side." That's one frightening name!

But Tom's journey would be easier because now there is a proper road through the Taklamakan. He still needed to carry a lot of water and be careful, but the desert wasn't nearly so scary these days.

The desert was, however, still lonely. Tom missed his family and friends. He met lots of interesting people on his ride, but because he couldn't speak their language he couldn't have a chat.

Instead, in the desert, he found himself talking to animals. This might sound crazy. But animals understood as much or as little of what Tom was saying as the people in China did. And vice versa.

"Maybe I am crazy," Tom said to a camel. "But if I don't talk to you, who can I talk to?"

The camel stared back, looking cross. It chewed some desert grass and drooled down its big droopy lips.

"Are you in a bad mood?" asked the boy.

The camel scowled and chewed. It was a Bactrian camel, twice as tall as Tom, with two big humps and a thick shaggy coat.

The camel did not reply. This conversation was not going very well. The camel blew through its big floppy lips and turned away.

"No need to be grumpy like that!" Tom shouted at the camel's retreating backside, which swayed from side to side as it walked.

"Why have you got the hump?!"

Tom laughed at his own joke. But the sound of his laughter was swallowed up by the lonely desert.

"Maybe I am going a bit mad," Tom said out loud. "First I'm talking to camels. Now I'm talking to myself …"

"That *is* a bit bonkers," replied Tom. With a start of surprise and a burst of speed, the boy picked up the pace to ride fast towards human company.

When you are crossing a desert you become used to certain colours. The sky is bright blue and the land is different shades of orange, red, yellow and brown. So whenever Tom came out of a desert he was surprised to see the colour green. If you have not seen trees or grass for a long time, green suddenly seems a very weird colour for much of the planet to be covered in.

The small oasis town he arrived at was built around a natural well of water, which meant that trees and crops could grow here. The plants smelled wonderful. Deserts have almost no smell, and Tom's nose twitched at the sweet smell of grass and flowers.

Vines grew over the streets, providing welcome shade from the fierce sun. The world became suddenly noisy: birds sang in trees, bees buzzed around fields and trees rustled in the breeze. Normally, a desert is a silent place except for the sound of the wind.

Tom was looking forward to finding people. He rummaged in his bags for the Chinese-language flash cards, then entered a café clutching the one that read: "I am really hungry. Please can I buy a big plate of food?"

The people chuckled, as always, as they watched Tom use his chopsticks. The boy was so hungry that he was even messier than usual. A waitress brought a large steaming bowl to the table. He shook his head, too full to eat more. But she was not bringing food.

The waitress pointed at Tom and wrinkled her nose in disgust. She thought that he was very dirty and needed to wash his hair! She pointed at the large bowl of hot water, then plonked down some shampoo.

Tom certainly was dirty: he had not had a shower for thousands of miles, and his hair was crusty with desert dust. He laughed. He had never washed his hair in a restaurant before!

Once his hair was clean, the waitress lent Tom a comb. He hadn't looked so shiny and smart in ages. With friendly farewells ringing in his ears, he cycled out of the oasis town smelling as fresh as a summer meadow.

It was summer now. The high, snowy Tien Shan mountains looked cold in the distance, but Tom was down low, where it was boiling hot. He was riding through one of the lowest and hottest places on Earth. The Turpan Depression is actually below sea level.

Tom gulped loads of water. His clean hair was a thing of the past as he became soaked with sweat. He dreamed of the sea. But Tom was further from the sea here than anywhere else on the planet. In a straight line, nowhere else in the world is further away from a beach than the Taklamakan Desert.

He rode past jagged hills striped with colourful rock which had eroded into hundreds of sharp gullies. The rocks were bright red and orange. As the setting sun shone, they glowed like flames. The Flaming Mountains – for this is what they are called – were a breathtaking sight.

Normally Tom dreaded riding uphill, but soon he was grateful; as the road climbed, the temperature dropped. He began following a small dirt track which he hoped would lead him over the mountains to the next country on his map, Kazakhstan. After a few hours of pedalling uphill, the temperature was perfect!

Unfortunately, he had not finished climbing. The road continued to ascend, and after an hour Tom was a little chilly. Two hours later, he was cold. Three hours later he was shivering, and the track was covered in snow.

But still the track rose, rising up towards a high pass. By the time he reached the pass the snow was as high as

THE BOY WHO BIKED THE WORLD

Tom's head! He pitched his tent and shivered unhappily. Yesterday he had been too hot. Today he was too cold.

The following morning, Tom needed to descend down the other side of the pass. It was too snowy to cycle, so he had to haul his gear by hand. There was too much to carry at once, so first of all he stumbled through the snow carrying his bike. He put the bike down and returned to collect two of his bags. Then he repeated the process over and over with the rest of his heavy, heavy bags.

By the end of the day Tom was wet, tired and in a very bad mood. In all, he had progressed fewer than two miles. As he shivered in his tent for a second night almost at the snow line, Tom looked forward to riding down into Central Asia and putting China far behind him.

The next day, he freewheeled down the track, away from the cold and towards warmer lands below. He zoomed through alpine meadows thick with flowers and purple lavender.

Cows watched the strange-looking boy who sang loudly as he cycled. Tom crossed bright blue rivers and waved at men saddling horses. Those final miles of China were fantastic. The third biggest country in the world had saved its best for last.

Tom had loved his China adventure, loved it as much as his Russian and Japanese ones. In all three of these fascinating countries he had eaten strange foods, met curious and friendly people, and learned a whole host of new skills. Woohoo!

10 phrases in...

	Russian русский	Japanese 日本	Chinese 中国
Hello.	Zdra-stvooj-te	kon nichi wa!	Ni hao!
My name's Tom	Mi-nia za-voot Tom	Boku no namae wa tomu desu!	Wo de ming zi shi Tom
What's your name?	A kak ti-bya za-voot?	Kimi no namae wa nani?	Ni de ming zi shi shen me?
I'm cycling round the world	Jah vi-la-si-pi-deest' ja poo-ti-sheh-stvoo-joo pa vsi-moo mee-roo	Boku wa jitensha de sekai isshuu wo shiterunda	Wo zai qi zi xing che huan you shi jie
I come from England	Jah iz Ang-lee-jee	Boku wa igirisu kara kitanda	Wo lai zi Yin guo

	Russian Русский	Japanese 日本	Chinese 中国
I am very hungry	Jah oh-chin kha-choo yest	Boku wa totemo onakaga suitayo	Wo fei chang e
I like bananas	Jah loo-bloo ba-nah-nɪ	Boku wa banana ga sukidayo	Wo xi huan xiang jiao
How much is it?	Skol-ka eh-tah stoh-yeet?	Sorewa ikura?	na ge Dong xi Duo shao qian?
Thank you very much	Bal-sho-ye spa-see-ba	Doumo arigatou	Fei chang gan xie!
Goodbye!	dah svee-dah-nɪ-ja pa-kah!	Jaane!	Zai jian!
	До свидания!	じゃあね！	再见！

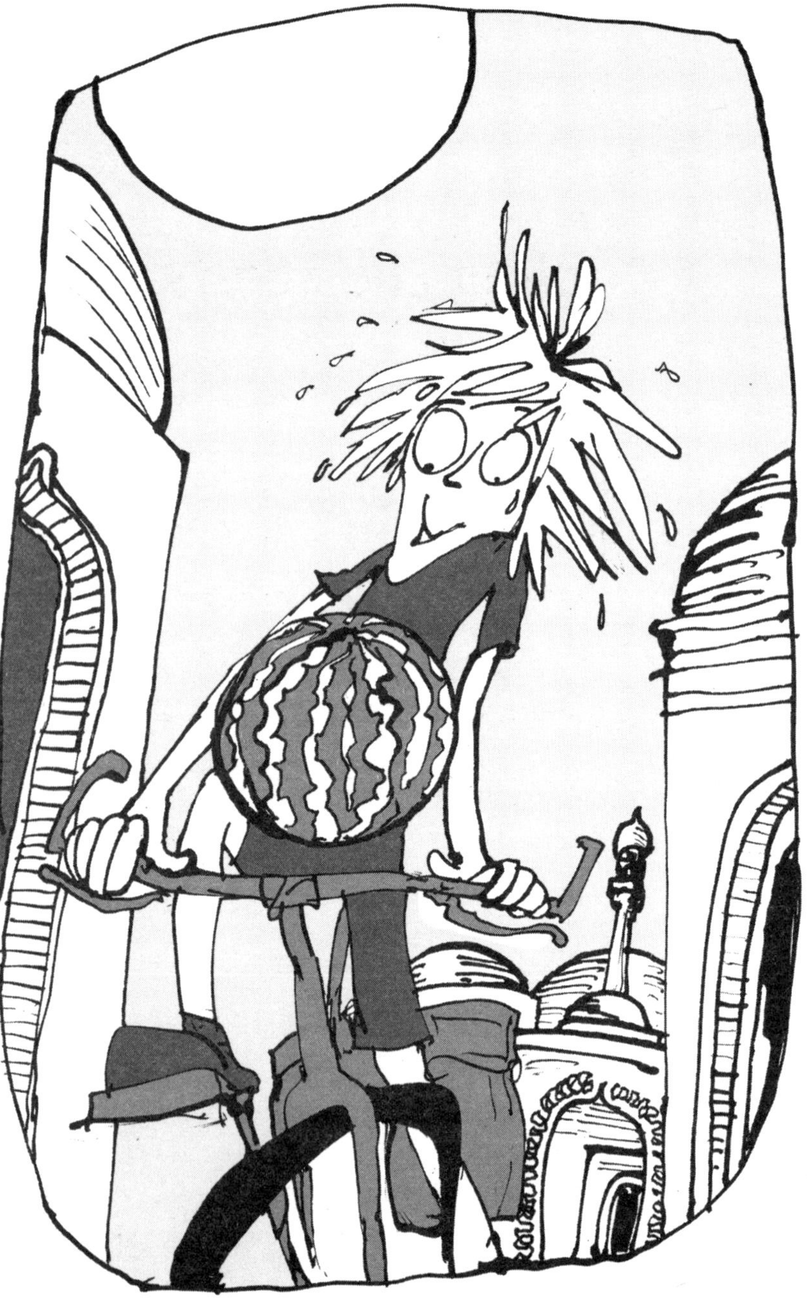

Cycling the Stans

Central Asia is made up of countries like Afghanistan, Kazakhstan, Kyrgyzstan, Tajikistan, Turkmenistan and Uzbekistan. "Stan" means "Land", so these countries are the Land of the Afghan people, the Land of the Kazakh people and so on. Central Asia's borders twist and turn around each other. There are even patches of one country that are completely surrounded by another country. It is a complicated part of the world.

The people in these countries speak many different languages (though most people speak Russian too, and all Muslims greet each other with the Arabic phrase *"Salaam aleikum!"* that Tom remembered from the Middle East). They are from many different backgrounds and wear a brilliant variety of funny hats.

Tom struggled even to spell some of the Central Asian countries, let alone pinpoint quite where they were on a map. He was learning a lot as he crossed them on his way towards Europe and home.

Today, heat folded around him in every direction. The sun pounded down on his head and pulsed upwards from the road. Smelly mopeds roared past, giving off clouds of fumes.

When the temperature grew unbearable, Tom pulled off the road and flopped down on the veranda of a café, hiding under the shade of some vines. A sympathetic café owner brought him iced water and refreshing pots of tea. Donkey carts pootled slowly past even in these hottest hours of the day and Tom raised a weary hand from the shade to wave to the drivers as they passed.

One constant in these countries were mosques of all shapes and sizes. Each has the symbol of a crescent moon on the roof. At dawn, mosques ring out with the call to prayer. Tom remembered this from his time cycling through the Middle East.

"Allahu Akbar! Allahu Akbar!"

"God is great! God is the greatest!"

This call is the same at all five prayers of the day, except at dawn when people are also urged to:

"Hurry to worship. Prayer is better than sleep!"

Though Tom had never been here, Central Asia felt more familiar than China. A lot of the signposts were written in the Russian script he had learned, so at least he could read roadsigns again. He recognised some words from Arabic and Russian, too, and some of the food was similar to Turkey's. Tom decided that his travels had taught him that all countries in the world are a mish-mash of their own culture – plus the good bits they've borrowed from other countries.

The calls from the mosques, the noisy motorbikes, the loud Arabic music playing in shops and cafés: it was fun to be in a busy bustle of people again after the emptiness of western China. Girls played with skipping ropes. Old men hunched over games of cards. Boys rode their parents' rusty bicycles, helping out with errands. The bikes were too big for them and to reach the pedals they had to sit on the crossbars instead of the seats. Butchers cycled between cafés on special tricycles kitted out with meat racks. Haunches of mutton dangled and swung to and fro as the butchers pedalled through the streets.

Each morning Tom began riding at first light, woken by the call to prayer from the nearest mosque. He liked cycling as early as possible before the day became too hot. But after only an hour he was forced to stop. He tried to keep going, but he could not help himself. For the air was filled with one of the most delicious smells in the world: freshly baked bread. He stopped riding and followed his nose to a village bakery.

Here, ovens are outside because it is too hot in the bakery. They are made from bricks and clay and about as big as washing machines. There is a big hole in the top of an oven and the insides are curved. The baker sticks the dough – which is round and flat like pizza – onto the hot inside wall of the oven until it is baked. Tom never quite understood how the bakers didn't burn their fingers.

Each baker decorates his dough with his own special pattern of pinpricked circles and swirls, then sprinkles it with seeds. Sesame, poppy or cumin seeds are the most common. Tom's bread was so hot that he had to juggle it between his hands as he carried it into the shade to eat.

His favourite time in the villages was the evening, after the heat had faded from the sky and the temperatures became pleasant again. People set up barbecues in the streets, lit by dangling lightbulbs. They fanned hot coals as skewers of lamb kebabs – *shashlik* – sizzled on grills.

Café owners wheeled pool tables out onto the pavement so that people could play outside in the cooler weather. Moths swirled round the lights as Arabic music swirled round the air. Tom sat happily munching kebabs, enjoying the discovery of this new part of the world that he had known nothing about until he had pedalled up and over that snowy pass from China.

Riding through Kazakhstan and Kyrgyzstan was brilliant. Herds of half-wild horses galloped across the endless, rolling grazing pastures called *jailoo*. Snowy mountains shimmered in the distance. Storks clattered their long bills from high, scruffy nests. Camels stared at Tom, their mouths constantly moving as they chewed. Tom had learned his lesson about trying to chat to camels, so he just waved as he passed.

Men worked the fields, swinging scythes to cut the long grass. Sweating in the heat, they loaded the grass onto gigantic trailers. This hay would feed their animals over the long winter months ahead.

At night, Tom camped in soft meadows filled with pink and yellow flowers; on lake shores; or in shaded, fragrant orchards. Apples originally came from Central Asia. In fact, the name of Kazakhstan's biggest city – Almaty – means "Father of Apples".

THE BOY WHO BIKED THE WORLD

Ladies with colourful headscarves and gold teeth smiled as he passed, and Tom stopped to buy fruit from them. They sold buckets of strawberries and pyramids of plums beside the roadside, alongside huge mounds of watermelons. Every few days Tom treated himself to a watermelon.

A sticky slice of watermelon is one of the most delicious things in the world when you are boiling hot. Tom dreamed of chopping a watermelon in half and shoving it onto his head like a cool, juicy helmet. The only downside of a watermelon is that they are massive and really heavy to carry on a bike.

Less delicious than watermelon were the drinks of *kvass* that Tom was sometimes offered. *Kvass* is a slightly fizzy drink made out of brown bread. *Kvass* was at least a bit nicer than *kumis*, a sour drink made from horse milk served inside a goat skin.

Each village had a communal water pump. Yanking a long metal lever up and down makes water glug from the spout. Whenever he saw one of these pumps, Tom stopped to fill his bottles. He learned the trick of pulling the handle up and down whilst his head was under the spout. The chilled water felt delightful on his hot, sweaty head!

SOME THINGS I'VE LEARNED ABOUT THE STANS...

- Afghanistan's national sport is "buzkashi", a mad game that involves players on horses trying to score a goal with the body of a (dead goat). People also enjoy flying kites and collecting wild flowers.

- Kazakhstan celebrates New Year on 20th March. There is an eagle on its flag. The first person who went into space, Yuri Gagarin was from Kazakhstan.

- Kyrgyzstan is traditionally a nomadic country. In the summertime many families move up to the high mountain pastures and live in yurts. They love horseback riding.

- Tajikistan has the highest mountain in central Asia. Ismoil Somoni Peak is 7,495 metres high. The Pamir Highway through these mountains is one of the most difficult but beautiful roads in the world.

- Turkmenistan's crazy old dictator, Turkmenbashi, renamed the month of January "Turkmenbashi". He ordered that both "April" and "bread" should be renamed after his Mum. He also banned gold teeth.

- Uzbekistan is one of only two "double landlocked" countries in the world. This means it is completely surrounded by countries that do not have coastlines themselves. Uzbekistan is not a good place to go for a beach holiday, but it's a great place to go if you like eating watermelons: they grow loads of them.

- Pakistan isn't usually one of "The Stans" but I like that its name came about because it is the combined land of these different regions: Punjab, Afghania, Kashmir, Sindh, and Baluchistan.

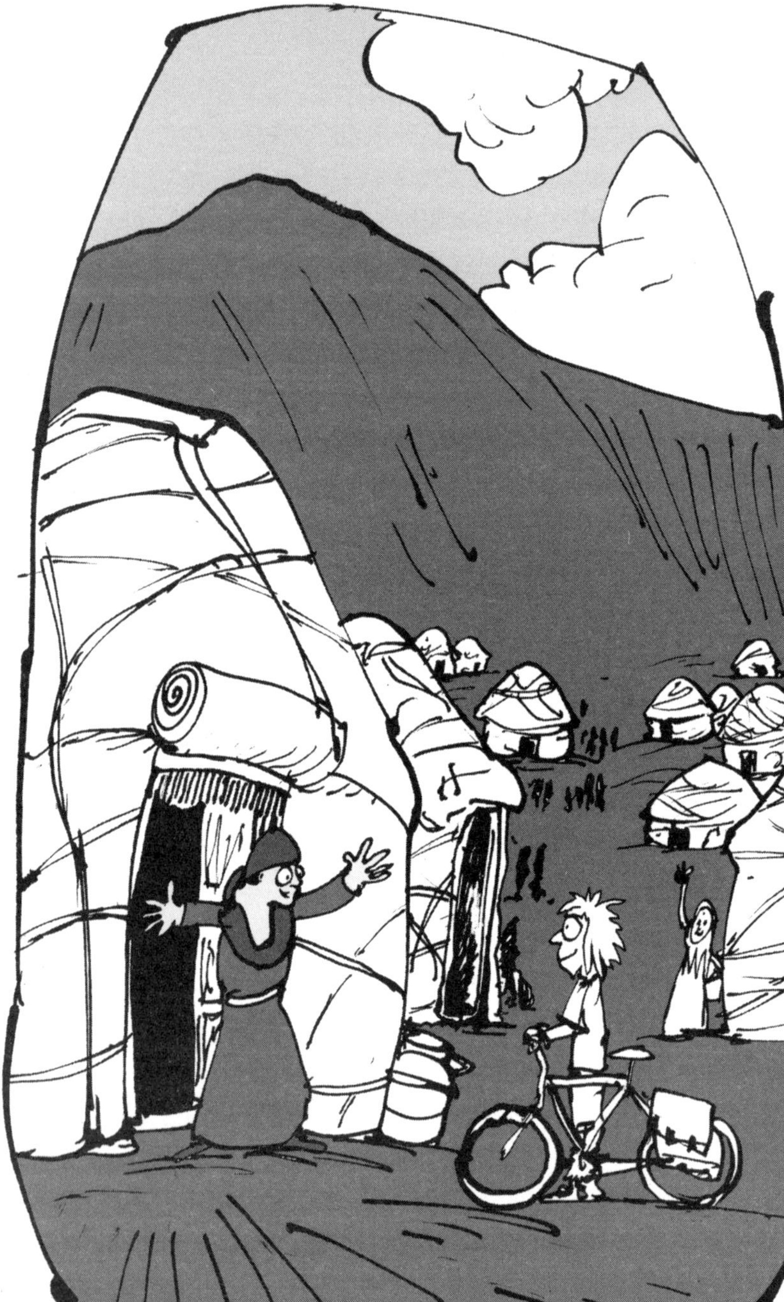

Nomads along the Silk Road

Many people in Kyrgyzstan are from nomadic backgrounds. They do not live in the same place all the time; instead they move around, following the seasons and the best grazing pastures for their precious animals. They were very curious about Tom's own nomadic adventures.

For thousands of years, nomadic communities across northern Asia have lived in yurts. A yurt is a tent, tall enough to stand up in, and big enough for a whole family to live in. They are quite similar to the traditional North American teepee.

Kyrgyzstan's flag is red with a yellow sun and in the centre of the sun is a red *tunduk*. A *tunduk* is the top of a yurt, the place where sunlight can enter.

Tom saw yurts dotted across the lush green pastures of Kyrgyzstan, looking like little white mushrooms in the empty expanses. One evening he was cooking his tea outside his own little tent when he spotted two horsemen galloping over the grasslands in his direction. The horses kicked up dust as they galloped.

Arriving at Tom's tent at an incredible speed, the horsemen heaved on the reins and skidded to a halt. The horses' nostrils flared as they panted for breath. The two men on the horses looked down at Tom. They smiled big smiles, filled with gold teeth, beaming out from beneath their brilliant big hats.

Tom smiled back and stirred his noodles. "Hi!" he said.

The horsemen were a father and son, called Taalay and Zhyrgal. They were expert horsemen and had looked tough and a bit frightening until they smiled. Indeed, they were tough men, for they both enjoyed playing *buzkashi*. In the olden days these games could go on for several days at a time and sometimes turn very violent!

But there was no violence now. Taalay and Zhyrgal had spotted Tom's tiny tent and ridden over in the last of the evening's sunlight just to say hello. Tom often felt like a nomad on his journey. He had no fixed home, and every day he packed up his life and moved on to somewhere different, to a new place to sleep, a new view to wake up to, and new horizons beckoning him onwards. So these three nomads had much in common. With smiles and sign language, Taalay and Zhyrgal invited Tom to come and spend an evening in their yurt.

Tom was happy to accept. It was nice to have company and he was curious to visit a yurt.

Taalay reached down, took hold of Tom's hand and helped him climb onto the back of his horse. And they were off. The race was on! Galloping into the sunset, hooves drumming the hard ground, dust flying, Zhyrgal shouting and whooping to make his horse go faster, Tom holding tight round Taalay's waist, Taalay urging more speed from his horse, the wind blowing back Tom's hair ... and all of them grinning at the fast-rushing, crazy speed. Too soon they arrived at the yurt and the race between father and son was over.

They climbed down from the horses and went inside to introduce Tom to all the family. Three generations lived inside the yurt. There was an old grandmother with a big smile and no teeth. She sat in the corner with a warm blanket over her legs. There was Taalay's wife, Anara – who was embarrassed for a visitor to arrive before she had finished cooking – and there were Zhyrgal's six brothers and sisters. It was a crowded but happy yurt!

Tom sat cross-legged on the floor beside the small, central cooking fire. The fire was fuelled by flat cakes of dried cow dung, and smelled exactly the same as so many campfires in Africa had smelled. Tom did his best to explain his adventures to this family who had travelled for their whole lives but had never been to school or left Kyrgyzstan.

Anara made Tom very welcome. To celebrate the boy's surprise appearance – which had caused a lot of amusement in the family – Anara cooked her favourite food just for Tom. He was treated to a meal of barbecued sheep's head, washed down with a drink of *kumis*, the horse milk in a goatskin. It certainly was different to a banana sandwich!

There are places in the world that people who love travel and adventure dream of visiting. That special place will be different for each person, but the dreaming and the excitement is the same. For some people the place might be Timbuktu. For others it might be New York, Nepal or New Zealand. Where do you dream of visiting?

For Tom, that place was Samarkand. Ever since he began his ride he had been excited about reaching Samarkand, which is located on the hot dusty plains of Uzbekistan. As he approached the legendary city, the sun was low in the sky, reflecting and glowing off the road. Tom kept pedalling, always a little further, along the golden road to Samarkand.

Samarkand is one of the greatest of the ancient Silk Road cities. Silk from China was first traded with Europe thousands of years ago. Travellers, explorers and merchants moved back and forth, carrying precious goods and making lots of money. Samarkand is famous for the beautiful blue domes of its spectacular mosques and its many great buildings. These days taxis buzz speedily round the incredible ancient monuments, but much of the city remains unchanged.

The markets are still busy and noisy, as they have been for centuries. As Tom squeezed through the crowds, past pyramids of apricots and pistachio nuts, around hat sellers and silk shawls and gigantic carpets, he liked imagining the famous explorer Marco Polo seeing many of the same sights that he was enjoying now.

The Boy Who Biked the World

Much of Samarkand today looks modern but if you get off the beaten track, you'll find ancient alleyways with walls made of mud and straw, and enormous old wooden doors that open into courtyards and vine-shaded gardens – exactly as Marco Polo described them 700 years ago.

Some things in the world change a lot. Other things stay the same forever. Both are good reasons to go out and discover the world for yourself.

Endless miles of sand and gravel stretched away to the horizon, shimmering with mirages in the furnace heat. Roadsigns warned drivers that camels might run across the road in front of them. Turkmenistan was the hottest place Tom had been since Sudan in Africa, even hotter than the Taklamakan Desert. Riding a bike when it is 45°C is hard work. (It's not as hard as -40°C though!) He was pouring with sweat all day long. Tom drank many litres of water and still hardly ever needed to pee.

Sometimes Tom passed ditches of water that farmers used to water their crops of melons. He jumped into each ditch in all his clothes, whooping with joy as he hit the refreshing water. He even left his shoes on. Soaked to the skin, he would then continue riding. The breeze felt deliciously fresh on his wet skin. But within minutes all his clothes would be completely dry again. The heat was cruel. It was hard to imagine that back in Siberia Tom had been desperately dreaming of hot days like this one.

It was a relief when the sun set and the world cooled down. Tom didn't sleep in his tent here. Even at night, the weather was warm and dry. He just unrolled his sleeping mat and lay down under the stars. When you sleep outdoors, even in your garden at home, your eyes become more sensitive and you see more and more stars until the sky seems to be bursting with them. Sleeping outside always feels like an adventure.

The Milky Way marched across the heavens and Tom noticed the moon sliding slowly across the sky towards the west each time he woke up and rolled over. Sleeping on a camping mat is not as comfy as a real bed so you wake up a few times every night. About an hour before dawn the sky in the east slowly began to lighten. It was time to get up – to make the most of the cool hours of the day.

Tom made a quick banana sandwich, glugged some water, and got riding. He didn't waste time brushing his teeth. By now Tom had learned the trick of brushing whilst pedalling, doing two jobs at once. If you brush your teeth for 4 minutes a day, that adds up over a year to 24 hours of tooth brushing. That meant that Tom could cycle about an extra 250 miles a year just while he was brushing his teeth!

On one of his best night's camping in Turkmenistan, Tom couldn't see any stars at all. He was camping on the edge of a crater. The desert was ablaze with bright light blotting out the stars. Turkmenistan has giant reserves of natural underground gas. The crater is filled with natural gas that is on fire so it looks like a huge cauldron of flames. The fire is about as big as a football pitch, and the blaze lights up the desert night. There is so much gas billowing up through the earth that this fire has been burning non-stop for 40 years. The fire is too huge to put out and so will keep burning until all the gas beneath the crater has burned off some time in the future. Local people call it the Door to Hell.

Tom was too excited to sleep that night. Not only was he camping next to a blazing crater, but ahead of him lay the Caspian Sea. Tom needed to cross the sea to get to Azerbaijan and Georgia. And beyond those countries lay Europe and home. With every turn of the pedals Tom was creeping a little closer to becoming the boy who really did bike all the way round the world.

MARCO POLO

Marco Polo is one of the most famous adventurers ever. He explored Asia 700 years ago. His adventures began when he was only 17 years old, and he was on the road for more than 20 years.

Marco Polo travelled from his home in Italy to China along the Silk Road. The Silk Road is a network of trade routes that has connected Europe and Asia for thousands of years. Precious silk was sold from China to Europe to make luxury clothes. Gold and other treasures went the other way to China. They had no maps back then and there were many difficulties along the way. It took Marco Polo four years to even get to China in the first place. Today, you can fly there in less than a day!

Marco Polo was the first European to visit Asia and write about it. His book was really popular as nobody back home knew anything at all about China. He was the first person to tell Europeans about things like paper money, a postal service, and gunpowder.

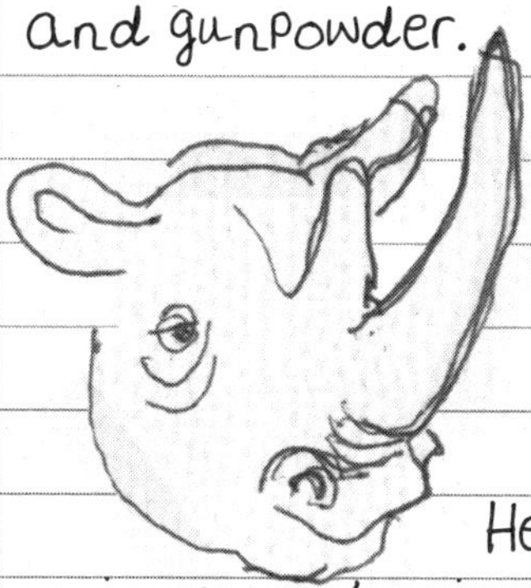

When he saw an Asian rhinoceros, Marco Polo actually thought that it was a unicorn!

He wrote that the people drink "mare's milk fermented to taste like white wine. It is very good to drink." But I've tried kumis and it is disgusting!

Lots of things that he saw are still around 700 years later.

Marco Polo has been inspiring adventurers for hundreds of years. Christopher Columbus carryied a copy of his book — which became known as "The Travels of Marco Polo" — when he sailed to America in 1492.

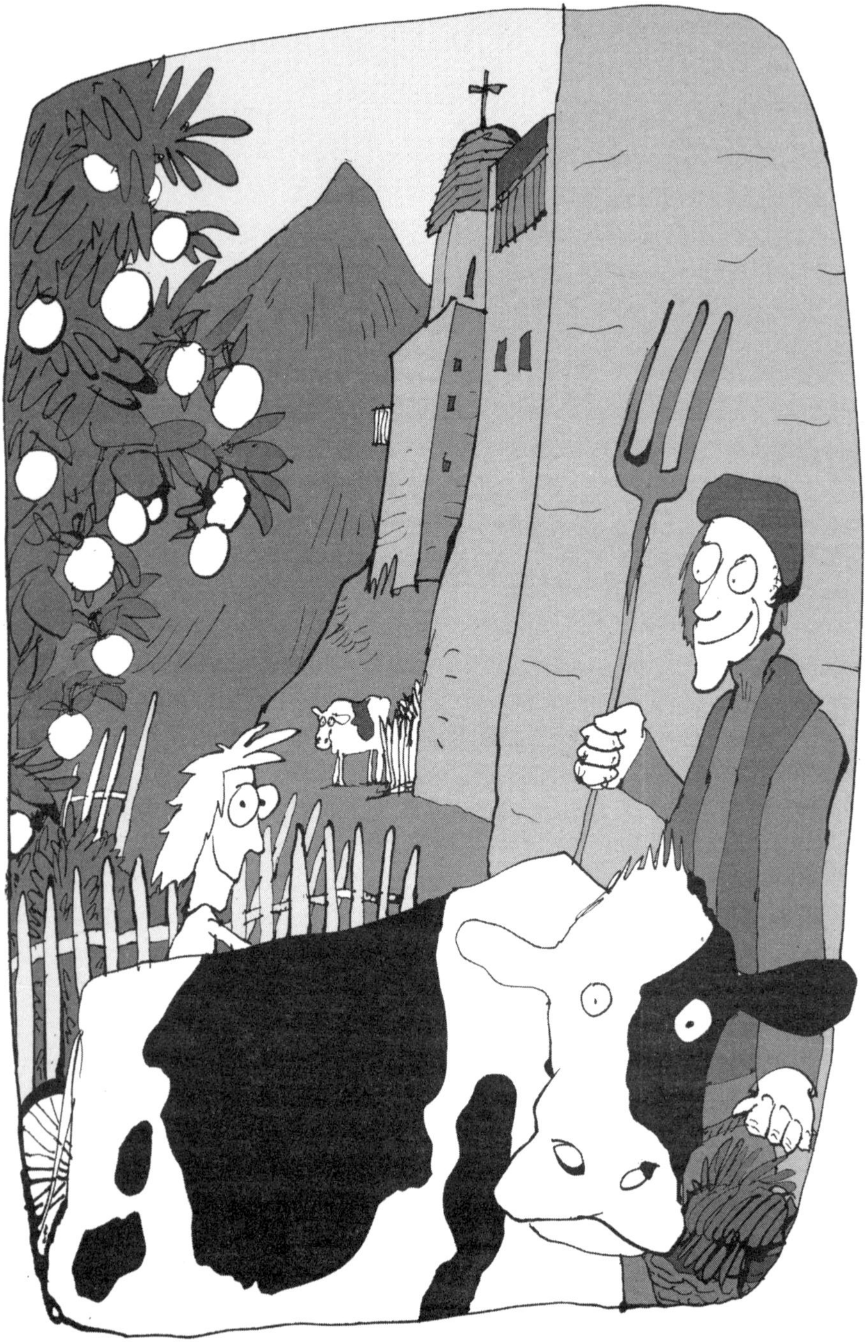

Goodbye Asia, Hello Europe

Travelling on an overnight ferry was a treat! Tom covered easy miles whilst he slept, *and* he got to spend the night in a soft bed instead of on the hard ground. When he woke in the morning the ferry was just pulling into the harbour in Baku. Tom climbed out of bed and looked out of the porthole with excitement. He cycled off the ferry and rode swiftly through the country of Azerbaijan, heading towards Georgia. He had a plan: he had been told about a food in Georgia called *khachapuri*, and he wanted to track it down.

Khachapuri is a cheese bread that is something between cheese on toast and a pizza. It is hot, soft and oozes cheese. Even better, people eat them for breakfast (and at most other times of the day). Every morning in Georgia Tom bought a *khachapuri* from a stall on the street. He ate it straight away and then bought another to eat later. It might sound greedy, but they were so delicious that Tom could not resist. He'd wait until he had left Georgia before returning to banana sandwiches.

ALASTAIR HUMPHREYS

Tom had to rely on his nose to hunt down his morning *khachapuri* because, once again, he was back in a country where he could not read a word of the local writing. Georgia has its own alphabet with 33 letters:

ა ბ გ დ ე ვ ზ თ ი კ ლ მ ნ ო პ ჟ
a b g d e v z t i k' l m n o p' zh

რ ს ტ უ ფ ქ ღ ყ შ ჩ ც ძ წ ჭ ხ ჯ ჰ
r s t' u p k gh q' sh ch ts dz ts' ch' kh j h

Tom, or თ ო მ enjoyed trying to spell different words he knew in the Georgian alphabet: it was like writing a secret code.

Most Georgians live in rural villages. Their homes are large cube shapes with steep roofs that extend out to make balconies and verandas on all four sides of the house. The gardens are filled with fruit and vegetables.

Georgia is a very green and fertile country. Cows amble slowly down quiet lanes. In each village are a couple of water pumps for those who do not have taps in their houses, and a small church. This is because Georgia is one of the very oldest Christian countries in the world.

Georgia is said to have been named for St George, the patron saint of many countries, including England, Portugal, Germany and Greece. There is a fable attached to St George, which goes like this:

Once upon a time there was a village called Silene. The village had only one well, but the well was guarded by a dragon. And whenever the village needed water they had to sacrifice somebody for the dragon to eat before it would let them have any water.

One day a princess was about to be sacrificed. Everyone was very sad. But a brave knight called George arrived on his horse in the nick of time. He galloped into battle and slayed the dragon with his sword. His heroism saved the princess and rescued the village. Despite all his courage, things ended quite badly though for poor George – later on in life, he had his head chopped off.

Tom cycled steadily through Georgia, winding up into the foothills of the Caucasus mountains. Off in the distance he spotted the sea. With a cheer he turned away from the mountains and began swooping down towards the shimmering water. The sun shone and the water looked lovely and blue, even though it was called the Black Sea. The road curved down through lush green tea plantations.

As Tom swooshed through the curves he thought of his Mum and Dad. They absolutely loved tea and got very excited whenever someone offered them "a nice cuppa". This whole mountainside planted with tea bushes was probably only enough to keep his parents going for a couple of weeks.

Tom squeezed hard on his brakes and slowed to a stop beside the Black Sea. After a quick swim he turned left and followed the coast back into Turkey. Tom rode along the seashore all the way to Istanbul. On his right was the sea, on his left side were rolling green hills covered with hazelnut trees. In the villages, all the flat space outside the homes were covered with hazelnuts spread out to dry in the sunshine. Tom camped on the beach at night and swam in the sea every day, often more than once. He hadn't smelled this clean in a long time!

Turkish bread, *ekmek*, is really good. It's a bit like a French baguette. As he cycled through Turkey, between handfuls of fresh hazelnuts, Tom invented a totally different food to eat: banana hotdogs. Here is the recipe:

- Slice open the *ekmek* lengthways
- Put one or two bananas lengthways down the bread (depending on how long the bread is)
- Do not squash it flat
- Eat

When Tom began his ride round the world so many thousands of miles ago, the first stage of his journey was to ride across Europe to Istanbul. To an inexperienced boy fresh from England, Istanbul had seemed to be the busiest, smelliest, most chaotic, exciting city ever. He was about to return to Istanbul.

Tom cycled to the shore of the Bosphorus. The Bosphorus is a narrow strait of water that separates Asia from Europe. This was the first place in the whole world – in his entire journey – that Tom had been to before. Imagine not ever seeing the same place twice for year after year, not knowing which way it is to the shops or what direction to take to leave town. Think about never knowing what is round the next corner or over the next hill. Do you think you would enjoy that? Tom loved it – all adventurers do. But he was also looking forward to being in more familiar places again.

Arriving at the Bosphorus was an important moment. He paused to take it all in. Old men sat peacefully on little stools holding fishing rods, just as Tom remembered. They still didn't seem to catch many fish, but they didn't seem to mind, either. They were happy chatting to their friends and feeling the warm sunshine on their faces.

Looking at the big ships sailing along the Bosphorus, Tom was delighted to have made it right across Asia. Asia was behind him. On the other side of the water lay Europe. Europe was the smallest and the easiest continent Tom was going to cross. He had already cycled it once so he knew he could do it again.

Tom wheeled his bike onto the little ferry for the short ride across the Bosphorus. Over the water was Istanbul's famous skyline of the Blue Mosque and Hagia Sophia, two buildings that he had visited last time.

"Goodbye Asia! I'm going to Europe. I'm on my way home now!" Tom shouted on the deck of the ferry into the breeze. A seagull whirled away in surprise at his loud voice. Having now cycled nearly the whole way round the planet, Istanbul felt much less chaotic, Tom found, than it had been the first time he visited. He knew that the city had not changed, but that he had changed during the course of his long adventure.

THE CAUCASUS

The countries of Azerbaijan, Georgia and Armenia are part of a region called the Caucasus. I really love going to places that I don't know much about - it feels more of an adventure that way.

Anyway, I found out that these are pretty interesting places.

I arrived in Azerbaijan by boat across the Caspian Sea. Azerbaijan was one of the first countries in the world to get rich from oil. They have a Professional Armwrestling Federation and the most mud volcanoes in the world (which bubble, stink and make lots of rude-sounding noises).

Georgia is the first Christian country I've ridden through in a long time and you see lots of beautiful churches on the hilltops. One of its most famous sons was (unfortunately) Joseph Stalin, who was responsible for killing millions of people in the Soviet Union. Otherwise, there are mountains to climb and ski, beaches, forests, lakes and delicious food - I'd love to come for a proper holiday!

Armenia and Azerbaijan have been arguing and fighting about an area of land called Nagorno-Karabakh for many years. Armenia is another beautiful, mountainous country, but sadly, I didn't have time to cycle though it. Armenia is a small country and there are far more Armenians living abroad than actually in Armenia itself. Also, if you go to school there, you have to learn chess in lessons!

STAMP
GEORGIA
BOSNIA
REPUBLICA DE
PANAMA
KAZAKHSTAN
PERU
MONTENEGRO
JAPAN
SIBERIA
CANADA
FRANCE
CHILE
USA

Pedal Power and the Final Push

This was it! The final stretch! Like in a running race when you see the finish line and suddenly find a new burst of energy, so too Tom rode faster and faster as he left the Bosphorus behind and rode into Europe. He was excited about getting home now – he only had about 3,000 miles left to ride. When you've ridden as far as Tom had, 3,000 miles doesn't seem very far any more.

Tom smiled to himself: he was actually going to make it round the world. When he began this trip he'd never thought he could do it; he just wanted to try his best and do more than he had ever done before. But now he knew that he really could make it to the end.

Tom pedalled through Greece, camping under orange trees on high cliffs above the blue Mediterranean sea. Glow-worms flashed in the trees above Tom's tent as he sucked an orange he'd picked from a tree. Cycling up through the limestone mountains of Macedonia, he was chased by some of the fiercest dogs he had yet encountered.

Tom loved dogs, but they did not always love him. All around the world, dogs enjoy chasing cyclists. Once, he had even been chased by a very fast dog who had only three legs but was desperate to try to bite Tom.

Sometimes when Tom shouted "go away!" at dogs, they stopped and gave up the chase. But he did not know how to shout "go away" in Macedonian. And it seemed that the dogs did not understand English. Certainly the louder he shouted the faster they chased and the more they snarled. They continued their hunt, barking loudly with savage teeth and drooling in a disgusting, frightening way. Tom was tiring fast. He was riding uphill, and even though he was pedalling furiously, the dogs were gaining on him, fast.

It was time for Tom's secret dog weapon. He grabbed his water bottle and squirted the dogs smack in their faces. The sudden burst of water shocked them into stopping. Tom seized the moment. He put on a final burst of speed and escaped from the pack! Heart beating and sweat pouring, Tom zoomed down out of the mountains, past Lake Ohrid and up the beautiful rocky coastline of Montenegro and Croatia.

By the time Tom arrived in Bosnia, the warm summer weather had gone. He hid from a heavy rainstorm underneath a tree. Sharing his tree was a very grumpy old lady with no teeth and one cow. Her face, wrinkled like a walnut, scowled with suspicion at the young cyclist. Perhaps she thought Tom was going to steal her cow.

Tom's hair was wild and long. His clothes were dirty and torn. The bags on his bike were battered and patched.

THE BOY WHO BIKED THE WORLD

His bike was almost worn out. *Tom* was almost worn out! So he did perhaps look like the sort of person who might steal a cow. But even though he had often daydreamed of having a pet for company, he had never thought a cow would make a good adventure partner.

As the young cyclist continued northwards, the leaves on the trees turned golden brown. The nights grew colder and the tent was crusted with frost when he packed it away in the morning. With his wheels spinning steadily through the miles, Tom passed the time by daydreaming about all the different things he had seen on his journey.

His teacher at school, Mr Field, used to get cross with Tom for being a daydreamer. Now that he had seen the whole world, his head was filled with a million new ideas for daydreams. When Tom returned to school, Mr Field was going to be furious!

One of the best things about adventures is that you learn lessons and make memories that will stay with you forever. Tom cycled along, thinking back over everything he had seen and done. Which of these things would you like to try one day? And what would you like to look up on the internet and learn about today?

Tom's favourite thing was food, so he thought about the meals that people eat around the world. Some of them made him drool with hunger, but others he never wanted to eat again. He thought of Maasai blood and milk, of goulash, *injera*, fly burgers and sugarcane, of chicken's feet, barbecued guinea pig, tacos and fried scorpions, *okonomiyaki* and *khachapuri, shashlik* and – of course – banana sandwiches. Although after all this time Tom was getting a bit tired of banana sandwiches.

He passed a few miles by trying to remember all the different ways he had learned to say "hello" on his ride. He practised saying them to all the cows and sheep he pedalled past. *Bonjour! Salaam aleikum, hola, zdrastvoojte, konnichiwa, ni hao, hallo ...*

He remembered rivers – the Danube, Nile, Yukon, Lena and Yellow. He thought of exciting creatures he had seen – the wild boar, elephant, albatross, king penguin, llama, flamingo, crocodile, grizzly bear and grumpy camels.

Many of Tom's happiest memories were from the people he had met along the way. Tom had met rich people and poor people, different races and religions, all sorts of shapes and sizes. There had been funny hats in Lesotho, Bolivia and Kyrgyzstan, and so many other interesting differences.

But there were other things that nearly everyone in the world had in common: they had all been excited by the idea of living adventurously, and everyone had been kind to Tom on the long road across Europe, Africa, the Americas and Asia. The world is a much better, kinder and happier place than it seems on TV. Tom thought that that was one of the most important lessons he had learned on the road.

And what a long road it had been! Tom understood now that he could cycle every single day for a hundred years and still not see everything in the world. How could anyone get bored when something new was waiting round every corner?

THE BOY WHO BIKED THE WORLD

And you don't actually have to jump on your bike and head for Africa to find those adventures. There are adventures waiting out there for everyone, every single day, wherever you live. It's just up to you to find them.

Tom thought about sweating through the Nubian and Taklamakan deserts, huffing and puffing over the Andes and Tien Shan mountains, the bizarre salt plains of Uyuni, the high, flat *altiplano* and the low, flat Turpan Depression. He had canoed the Yukon River, shivered through Siberian snow, pedalled across the *jailoo*, ridden past baobabs and through a giant redwood tree. And now he was riding home.

Tom crossed the border into France, which meant that there was only one more country to go. Ride, eat, sleep. Repeat. Tom was on a mission now. He was riding home as fast as he could, excited about seeing his friends and family again. Ride, eat, sleep. Repeat. His socks smelled astonishingly bad. They smelled like some of France's famous cheeses.

Tom dreamed of putting down his bike for a while and enjoying his Dad's tasty cooking. If he ever saw a banana sandwich again he thought he might scream. When Tom had ridden through France at the start of his ride, every day had been new and different and difficult. But by now he was so fit that pedalling a hundred miles was almost effortless.

And all the other daily tasks of cycling round the world were a comfortable habit now – finding food, water and a safe place to sleep, asking for directions, repairing things when they broke, setting up camp. Tom feasted in his tent in a field near Paris. He ate crumbly croissants and ham and cheese – all with a brilliant view of the Eiffel Tower. French food was delicious, except for the bits that smelled like his feet.

When you get near to the end of a big, big journey it's normal to start to feel impatient. It's like when you go on holiday – the outward trip can be quite exciting. Nothing's better than winding down the window and letting the wind blow back your hair. You look out eagerly, trying to be the first to see the sea. You are not yet bored of games or of your parents' music.

But coming home from a holiday is boring. The fun is over and you just want to get back. You miss things from home that you don't normally take much notice of. You are tired. You want to be home.

So imagine how Tom was feeling now! He had been away from home for so long. He had ridden through 60 different countries. He had crossed five continents. He had pedalled 46,000 miles. That was almost far enough to go all the way around the equator, not once but twice! Now Tom just wanted to get back to England. He pedalled faster. The faster he rode, the sooner he would be home.

Tom boarded the ferry to cross the sea from France back to England. Soon the white cliffs of Dover gleamed in the sunshine.

The Boy Who Biked the World

"Hurry up! Hurry up!" Tom wanted to shout to the ferry captain. He stood up on the top deck. The wind whipped his hair and the autumn air was cold. But Tom didn't notice. His heart was beating quickly with excitement. Tom had nearly finished this enormous adventure – the adventure nobody had thought that he could do.

To his surprise, Tom felt tears welling in his eyes. He was happy, so why was he crying? But as well as being happy, he also felt sad. Tom had met brilliant people on his journey. He had seen amazing things. He had been to wonderful places. And it was nearly over. He was going to miss cycling round the world. Tom had very mixed feelings about the end of his adventure as the ferry arrived in the harbour.

"Welcome back!" shouted the lady from the ticket office window as Tom zoomed down the ramp into England. She had handed Tom a free ferry ticket all those years ago because his plans had sounded so crazy and she wanted to help a little. "I still think you're bonkers, but well done!" she said.

Tom waved, smiled and cycled home.

LAST POSTCARD HOME

Dear Mum, Dad and Lucy,

Not long now till I get back home! Europe has got so much squashed together in all these little countries. I saw the Acropolis on a rocky hilltop in Greece. It's 2,500 years old and really impressive. I swam in Lake Ohrid in Macedonia and in the sea outside the famous walled city of Dubrovnik in Croatia. Croatia's money (the kuna) is named after a little animal like a ferret!

I pedalled up through the hills of Bosnia and over a really high bridge in a town called Mostar. Some brave people were jumping off it into the river far below! Sarajevo is a pretty city, but there was a terrible war here once. There are many scars on the streets from exploding bombs. These have been repaired with something red and are called "Sarajevo Roses" so that nobody forgets the war.

I followed a valley up the Soča River, the bluest river I have ever seen.

A: Mum, Dad and Lucy
Adresse: My Home
My Street
Yorkshire
ENGLAND

The cathedral in Milan was very impressive, but I mostly liked it because it was a shady spot to rest and eat yummy Italian ice cream!

The Alps were my last range of mountains in this whole adventure. I definitely find it easier to ride over mountains now than I did when I first set out on this trip!!

I'm excited about seeing you all again, and I'm riding as fast as I can.
Love, Tom

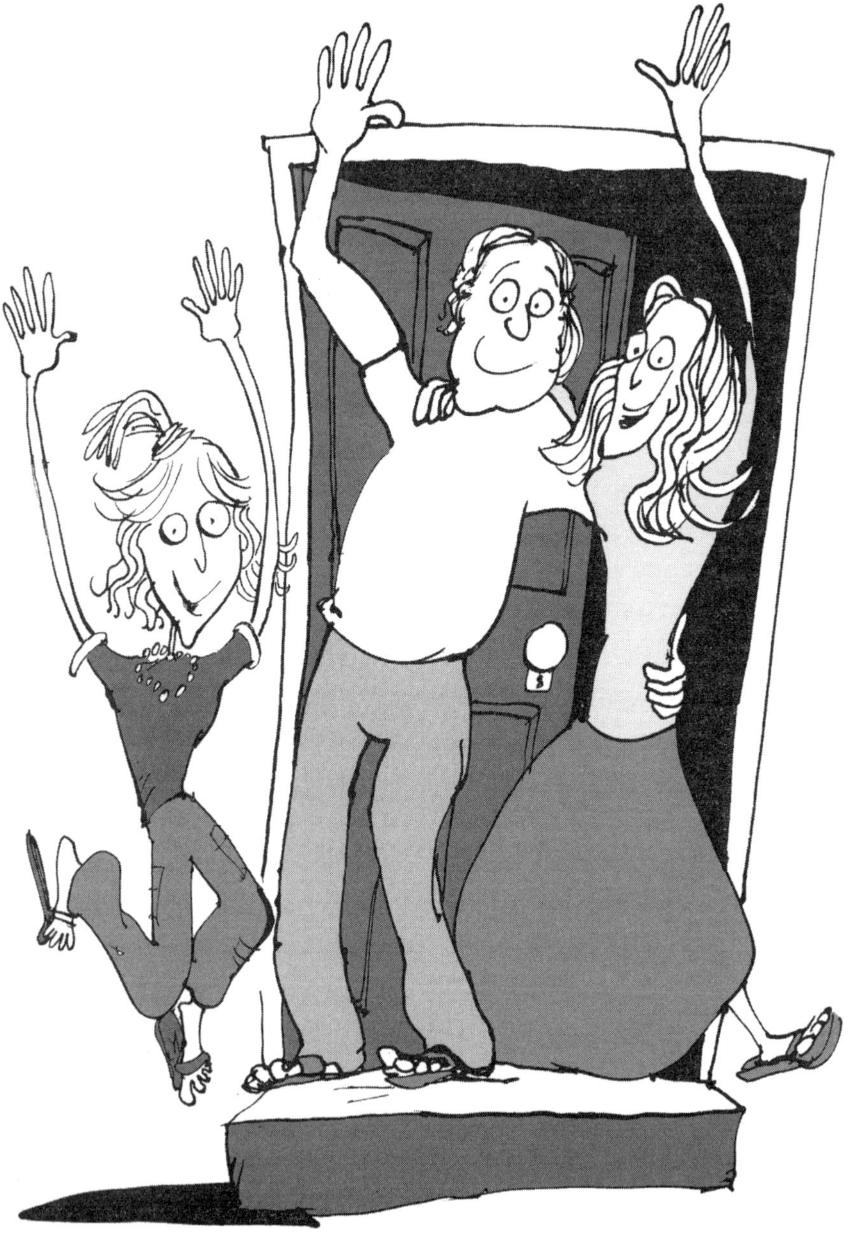

Round the World and Home Again

One of the best reasons for visiting other places is that when you come home you understand where you live a little bit better. All the things that we think are totally normal are actually a tiny bit different in every country in the world. Tom noticed so much more now, seeing his own country again for the first time in so long. The roadsigns look different to everywhere else in the world. The traffic lights beep differently. Shops smell different and sell slightly different things. The trees and fields look different. People think and behave differently.

Tom had seen so many things on his ride. He understood now how lucky he was in his life at home. His life was easier, safer, happier and more luxurious than most children in the world can ever dream of. He had also learned that the world is a good place. Nearly everyone is more or less a good, decent person. Now that Tom had seen the world for himself he knew that despite the bad, sad, terrible stories he saw on the news, there were so many good people who had looked after him in the villages, towns and cities of 60 different countries.

Tom had found out a lot about the world. But his ride had shown him even more about himself. He knew now that he was capable of doing more than he had ever imagined. He hadn't honestly thought that he'd get all the way round the world, but he had begun to do it anyway. Beginning something is a really good trick. It's the best way to become good at it. If you just wait around hoping to become an expert on something, then you'll never get good. You'll never achieve anything difficult. Beginning is the best way forward. It's far better to try something and fail at it than to be too scared to even begin it in the first place.

Cycling round the world had made Tom a more confident boy. Nowadays he enjoyed trying new things. He was less worried about the prospect of failing. He was more willing to ask people for help, to try his very hardest, but also to have fun. Having fun might be the most important part of any adventure.

———🚲———

One morning Tom woke up and thought "this is the last day". He climbed out of his sleeping bag for the last time. He packed away his tent for the last time. Tonight he was going to sleep in his very own bed. He grinned at the idea. Tom liked – even loved – his tent, but he was definitely looking forward to a soft bed and a big duvet. He was also looking forward to a steaming hot shower. He might even throw away the pants he had been wearing all the way around the world, and treat himself to a clean pair. Life was great!

Tom pushed his bike out of the wood he'd camped in and out onto the road. He began pedalling. The last day felt strange. It was the first time in the whole world that Tom had not needed a map to show him the way ahead. He recognised places as he passed them. He knew what he was going to see when he reached the top of a hill. Tom rode fast, remembering how slow he had been when he first began this trip, wobbling on his bike as he set off ever so slowly to try to ride to Africa. If you ride a bike every day you will get very fit and strong. It is a magical feeling.

We all live on the road to Africa. Look out of the window now. Can you see a road? That road, that very one, is the road to Africa. Those two lanes will take you anywhere – to Africa, to China, or to anywhere you dream of going. All you need to do is to make a plan, and to begin. It may not be right now; it may not even be for a few years. But you can start dreaming of adventures today. And you can start seeking out adventures close to home right away. You don't have to cycle round the world to have an adventure. Anyone can find somewhere to explore near their home. Maybe you could camp out in the garden, make hot chocolate in the woods, or even just climb a new tree.

But if you do one day think big and decide to ride down that road, you'll always be glad that you did. Turn left at the end of the street. Turn right at the next traffic lights. And then just go – this is the road to adventure. And it is up to you to choose if you will take it or not.

Anyone *could* cycle round the world. But not many people actually *do*. Tom made the choice. That is the only difference between him and all the other boys and girls at his school, between people who *dream* of adventures and people who *have* adventures. *You* could cycle round the world too if you choose to, or have a million other types of adventures. Will you?

It was late afternoon. Almost tea time. The sun was low in the sky as Tom rode the final hill. The last hill in the world. From here on, it was all downhill. Left at the traffic lights. Second right. Just a little further on. And then Tom saw it. His house. Home.

His Mum, Dad and Lucy stood outside, waiting. At the top of his voice Tom shouted, "I'm home!" and pedalled as fast as he had ever ridden in his life.

Tom's family heard him shout. They began cheering and jumping up and down with excitement when they saw him. Tom zoomed up to the front door and skidded to a stop, just as he had always done. He leapt off his bike and into the arms of his family, who gave him the biggest and best hug of his whole life.

"Welcome home, Tom!" said his Mum.

"You're the boy who biked the world. I'm proud of you," said his Dad.

"You stink!" said Lucy.

They all laughed.

"Come inside. I've made your favourite meal," said

his Mum. "You must have missed it while you were away on all your many adventures."

"Thanks, Mum," replied Tom. "I'm really hungry."

They walked through the front door and into the kitchen.

There, on the kitchen table, was a plate.

And on the plate was a towering pile of banana sandwiches.

Tom groaned.

It was good to be home.

MY LIST OF "-ESTS"

- Longest Day in Distance: I cycled 150 miles in one day in Peru – (brilliant!)
- Shortest Day in Distance: I carried my bike by hand through Chinese snowdrifts in China. Only two miles covered – hard!
- Highest Point: 4,900m, the Andes.
- Lowest Point: -392m, the Dead Sea. Jordan is below sea level; the water is so salty that you float like a cork!
- Longest Time at Sea: 24 days sailing the Atlantic.
- Furthest away from the Sea: near Urumqi, China.
- Hottest: 45°C, Sudan and Turkmenistan. It's horrible cycling in such heat.
- Coldest: -40°C, Russia. It's REALLY horrible cycling when it's so freezing cold.
- Steepest Road: 35% gradient, Lesotho. I had to push my bike.
- Longest Uphill: 2 days riding uphill – common in the Andes.

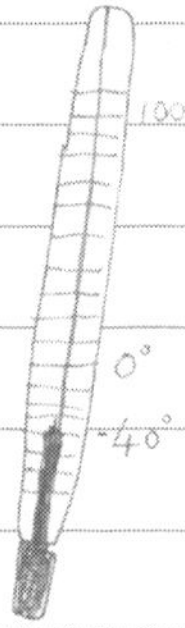

- Longest DOWNHILL: 50 miles, Peru. Fantastic!
- Most Food Carried: 10 days, Alaska and Siberia.
- Most Water Carried: 18 litres, Argentina.
- Most Punctures in a Day: 15, Bolivia. I cried!
- Most VOMITS in a Day: lots, Turkey. I was really sick but had to keep riding. I was sick all through the night, too. In the morning a dog stole my shoe, which I eventually found in some bushes. Not a good day.
- Longest Ride WITHOUT A BREAK: every day for a month, 2,600 miles through China.
- Longest Time WITHOUT A SHOWER: one month, China. It was then that the lady in the café made me wash my hair.
- Longest Time without a Conversation: 8 days, Argentina and Chile. I chatted to myself a lot!
- Furthest North: 70°, Alaska.
- Furthest South: 56°, Argentina.
- Furthest East: 179°, 59' 59' E Pacific Ocean.
- Furthest West: 179°, 59' 59' W Pacific Ocean.

FIND OUT AND COLOUR IN - FLAGS

Here are the flags of a few of the 60 different countries I visited in my cycle round the world. Look in books and search the web to help you colour them in.

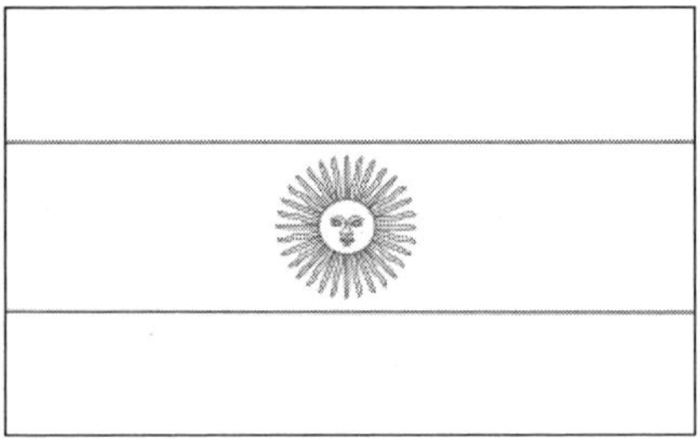

Argentina

Canada

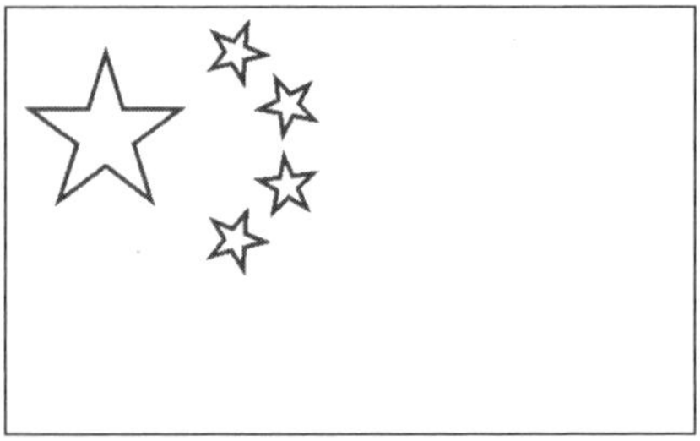

China

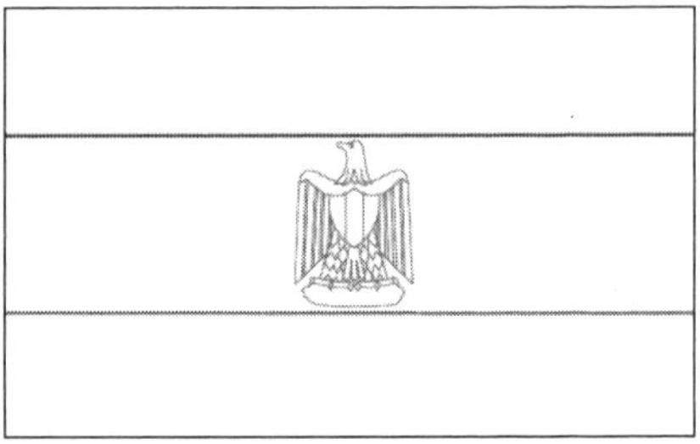

Egypt

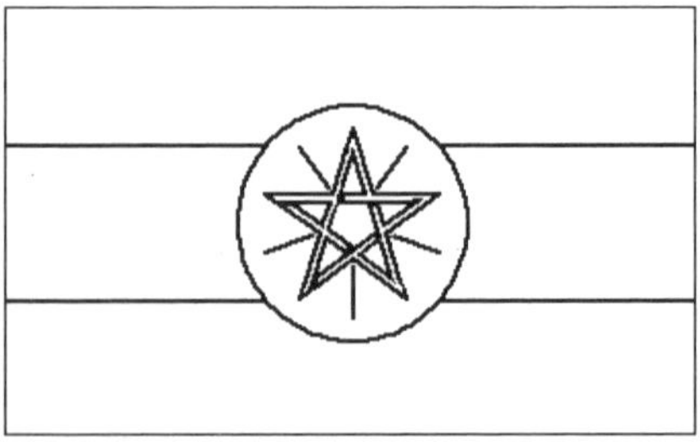

Ethiopia

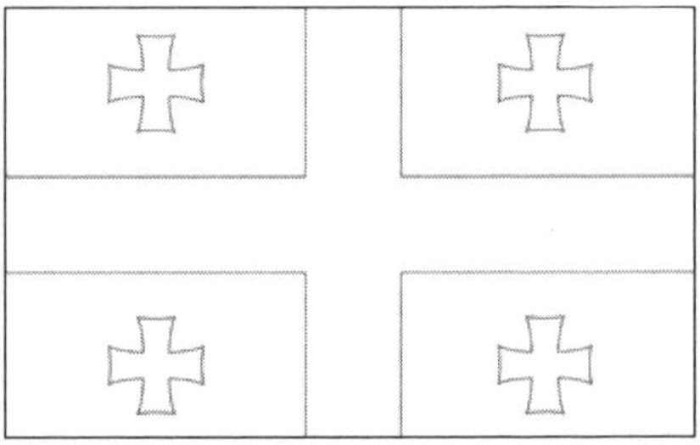

Georgia

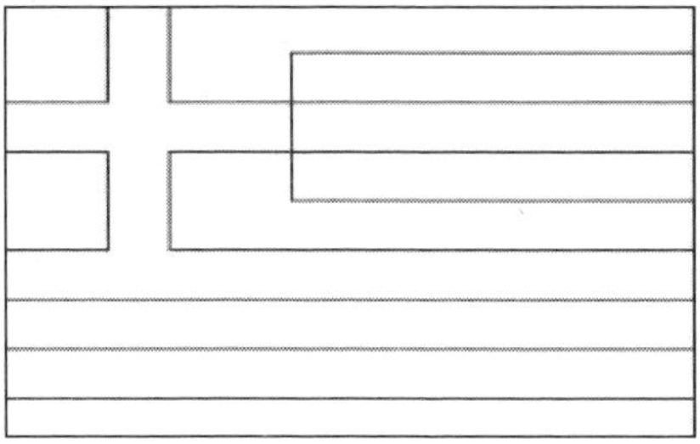

Greece

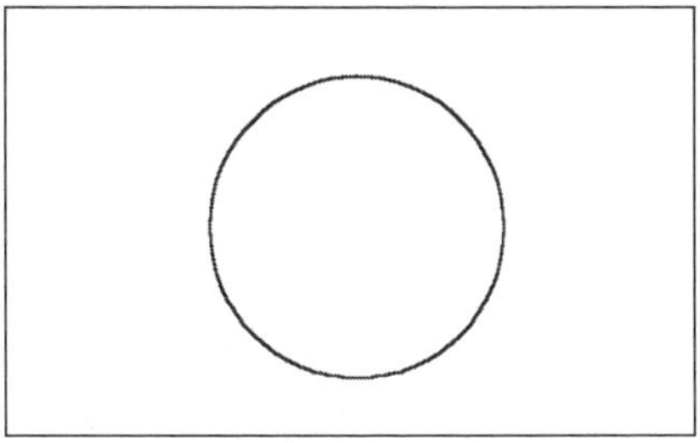

Japan

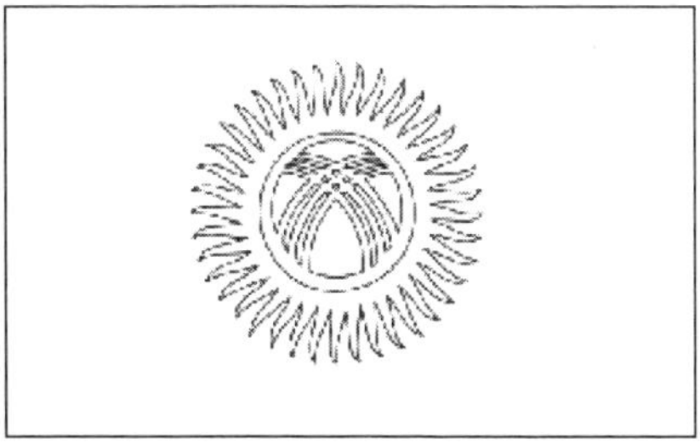

Kyrgyzstan

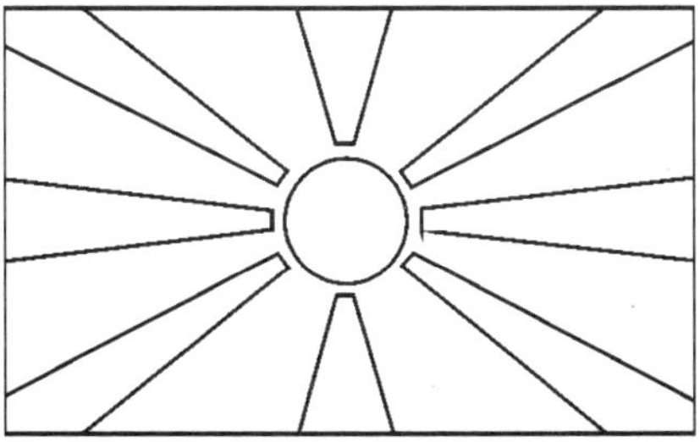

Macedonia

Russia

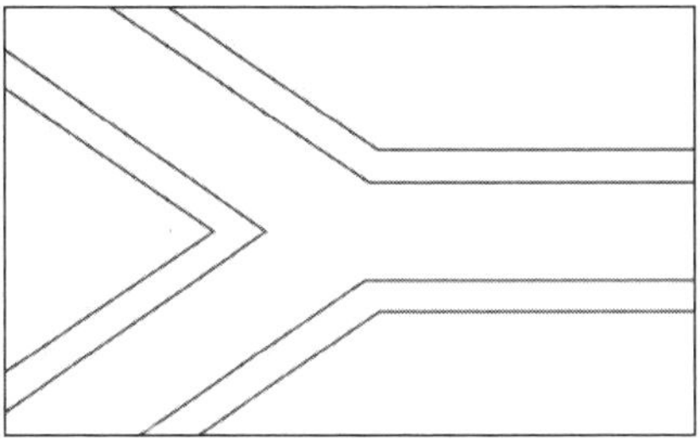

South Africa

UK

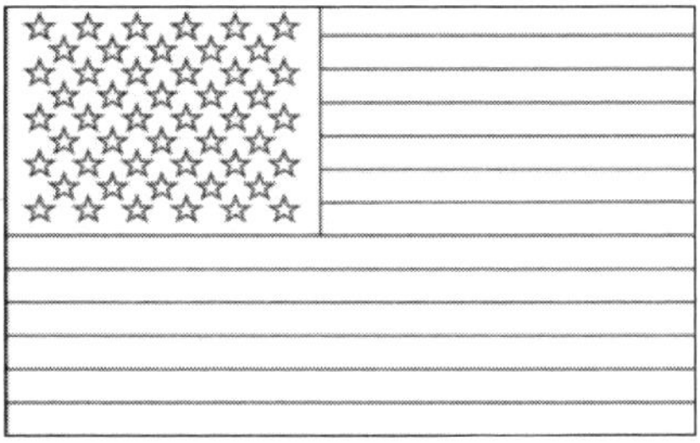

USA

YOUR ADVENTURE JOURNAL

Start your own adventure and keep a journal - it's fun to read and remember everything. I've written some questions to help you make a start:

What sort of adventure would you like to have? Hot or cold; long or short; cycle, hike or somehow else?

Which environments would you like to explore? Deserts, mountains, the sea ...

What country would you like to visit?

Which Wonder of the World (ancient or modern) would you like to see?

What gear would you need to take?

What difficulties would you need to overcome on this adventure?

A trip closer to home can still be an adventure... Here are a few thoughts to help you work out a plan:

What is the highest hill within an hour of your home?

How would you get there?

What would you need to take with you?

Who would you like to climb that hill with?

When are you going to go and do it?

Acknowledgements

Thank you to Martha, Dan, Jenny and Tom for all their hard work on the book.

Spasiba, arigato and *xie xie* to Katerina, Mitch and Stefen for helping with translations.

And thank you to you – the readers of this series of books. Your enthusiasm is wholly responsible for making me sit down at a computer for long enough to write the story.

About Eye Books

Eye Books is a small independent publishing house. The team who works at Eye Books passionately believes that the more you put into life the more you get out of it.

Eye Books celebrates 'living' rather than existing. We publish stories that show ordinary people can and do achieve extraordinary things.

We are committed to ethical publishing and try to minimise our carbon footprint in the manufacturing and distribution of all Eye Books.

Follow Eye Books on Facebook, Twitter @eyebooks and our website www.eye-books.com

www.eye-books.com

eye books
Extraordinary Things Done by Ordinary People

About the Author

Alastair Humphreys is an adventurer, blogger, author and motivational speaker. He regularly visits schools to talk about his adventures.

Alastair's quest for adventure began young. Aged eight, he completed the Yorkshire Three Peaks challenge and at 13 he did the National Three Peaks in 24 hours! At 14 he cycled off-road across England.

At university, Alastair trained to become a teacher. But adventure took over! Alastair has now cycled round the world, raced a yacht across the Atlantic Ocean, canoed 500 miles down the Yukon River and walked the length of the holy Kaveri river in India. He has run the Marathon des Sables, crossed Iceland by foot and packraft, rowed across the Atlantic Ocean, and walked across the Empty Quarter desert.

More recently Alastair has been encouraging people to seek out adventure close to home. The 'microadventures' idea saw Alastair named as one of National Geographic's Adventurers of the Year.

Alastair is always blogging and tweeting about his adventures, big and small. Visit his website www.alastairhumphreys.com to see what he is up to and follow him on social media.